ONCE UPON A COUNTESS

LOVE & DEVOTION SERIES #2

JAMIE SALISBURY

The carriage, pulled by four perfectly matched white horses, drew up outside the towering classical façade of Clevedon House, the London residence of the Duke of Clevedon. If it weren't for the fact that the duke was a close friend from their days at Eaton and Cambridge, Parr would have declined the invitation. This evening, however, was important to Clevedon. It was the first dinner party held by the recently married duke and duchess, and Parr could never refuse Clevedon. The duke had assured him the affair would be small, knowing Parr disliked large, crowded events.

His own sister, Alexandria, reminded him he needed to host some sort of social event as well. As the Earl of Wexford, Parr needed to expand his social horizons beyond White's. Alexandria was of the opinion that he needed a new wife and promised him she would put together a tasteful affair. He'd escaped a lengthy discussion over whom he should invite for the time being. That had proved easy enough. He'd merely promised her he would give the matter serious consideration.

Clevedon and his charming wife, Savannah, Her Grace the Duchess of Clevedon, were waiting inside the door, in the grand hall. His friend the duke had fallen head over heels in love with the charming American and her young son. A tale to be savored another time. Wexford needed to focus his attention on his hosts.

"Clevedon," he murmured before turning his attention to the duchess. He bowed slightly. "You look as beautiful as ever, Your Grace."

"Thank you, dear Wexford, and thank you for accepting our invitation. My husband says you're not fond of large social events."

He smiled. "He would be correct. I find I dislike the crush of the endless balls and soirees."

"May I tell you a secret?" she asked with her prominent American accent. "I'm not fond of them either, so your secret is safe with me."

Clevedon cut in. "I believe you'll be fine, Parr. There are several guests you know, and my wife managed to keep the affair small."

Parr nodded and again gave the duchess a slight bow before he walked off in the direction of the drawing room. Champagne was being served, and he took a flute from the tray of a passing footman. Taking a long sip, he walked through the doors.

He found there were, by his count, ten couples in total, plus one young woman who appeared to be on her own, without an escort. Perhaps one of the duchess's friends or some distant relation of the duke's. In either case, he was intrigued. The young woman obviously had a season or two behind her. She seemed comfortable conversing with those around her.

She was an exquisite creature. Her ginger hair was swept

up off her neck. A long, luxurious neck, one that was made for kissing. Pearls adorned that beautiful neck, and she wore a deep-sapphire-colored silk gown. She looked like a queen or, in his case, a countess. That was absurd. He wasn't looking for a wife, even though everyone told him it was past time. He'd been in mourning for his late wife, Matilda, for over a year, and until this evening had never given the matter any thought.

Clevedon came to his side, observing the festivities. The candlelight caught the reddish highlights that shimmered through his golden-brown hair. His muscular frame made him stand out from other men, showing he wasn't afraid of hard work, something his fellow peers avoided. "I see you've found Lady Clare."

"Lady Clare?"

"Yes, the beauty in the dark blue gown."

Parr finished his champagne and took another from one of many footmen. "Who accompanied her?"

"No one. She's my cousin on my mother's side. She was raised in Scotland and France."

"Really? That's fascinating. So she's not betrothed?"

"No, which is why my aunt sent her to London."

Parr arched a brow and smiled. "Tell me about her, and yes, you must introduce us."

"Don't worry, I will. I believe my wife has seated the two of you together for dinner."

"Excellent. I knew there was a reason I liked the duchess."

"Come. I want to acquaint you with a few gentlemen I don't believe you know, and I'll make sure you are introduced to Lady Clare before we go in to dinner."

"Excellent. What else can you tell me about her before we're introduced? You said she was your cousin."

Clevedon finished the remainder of his champagne and placed the flute on a nearby table. "As I said, she's my cousin and was raised in Scotland and France. Her father, my uncle, is the Duke of Renfrew. Clare is proficient in French, Gaelic, and Italian, she can ride better than most men I know, she paints, and is far more proficient than most other young ladies on pianoforte."

Parr nodded as he listened. "What of her temperament?"

His friend smiled ever so slightly. "She is a delight to be around so long as you don't rile her. She's known for her fierce Scottish temper and a tart tongue."

"Lady Clare sounds quite interesting. I look forward to getting to know her better."

"Let me introduce you before we get bogged down in some political discussion with the men."

They walked across the drawing room to where Lady Clare stood between Viscount Newton's wife, Lady Newton, and Countess Taylor. Her husband, the Earl of Taylor, was well known as a successful land baron with property throughout England and Wales.

"Ladies, I would like to present Parr, the Earl of Wexford," Clevedon said. "Wexford, I believe you already know Countess Taylor and Lady Newton."

"I do. Ladies, nice to see you this evening."

"Wexford, may I present my cousin, Lady Clare."

Parr nodded and took the hand Lady Clare offered. "Lady Clare, I'm pleased to meet you."

She studied him for a moment, her dark green eyes sizing him up. "I'm sure you are, Lord Wexford. Everyone is."

Wexford arched a brow. "I beg pardon, my lady?"

Did she actually roll her eyes at him? Clevedon hadn't mentioned her being a snob.

Lady Clare opened her fan, then closed it. "My father, the Duke of Renfrew, is quite wealthy, and unfortunately, I find most men use me as a way to get into my father's good graces."

"I can assure you I live quite comfortably, and what your father has or may not have is not my concern."

"How refreshing, Lord Wexford. A man with no interest in my father's money."

"If you ladies will excuse us," Clevedon said. "Lord Hemsley is beckoning us."

Wexford bowed. "Ladies, a pleasure as always. Lady Clare, it has been good to meet one of Clevedon's Scottish relations."

The two men strode across the room toward a small group of gentlemen, Lord Hemsley among them.

"So that's your cousin."

The edge of Clevedon's mouth curved up. "I warned you. She thinks any man who shows interest in her simply wants to get close to the duke."

"Her tongue is enough to scare off most men."

"Indeed. She's had two proposals, both of which she refused, and her father didn't approve of one in any case. He allowed her the other refusal. And yet, as I said, her father wishes her wed."

Wexford snorted. "I do believe I've heard of your cousin. Her dowry's reportedly the largest in all England and Scotland."

"Her name and dowry precede her. I'm afraid it's worn on my cousin."

"I can see where it might."

They neared the group of men, stopping just short of joining them. "You'll get to know her better at dinner,"

Clevedonsaid. "Just don't bring up money, and you should be safe from her wrath."

"I'll try to remember that." Parr glanced across the room and saw the duchess had joined the group. Unfortunately, Lady Clare's back was to him, and he couldn't see her face. Dinner would commence shortly, and he would have his chance to get to know the lady better then.

———

As this was the duchess's fist official dinner party, the meal would be a long-drawn-out affair. Dinner began with a delicate turtle soup.

From the moment he sat down next to Lady Clare, Parr knew his evening would be anything but dull. She didn't look at all surprised that they had been paired together. She sat quietly for a moment before speaking after he'd acknowledged her as he settled himself in his chair

"Lord Wexford. Imagine that, the only two unmarried people at this dinner party being seated together. How curious."

"I'm sure Her Grace thought you'd rather be seated with me rather than, say, Lord Hemsley."

She picked up her wineglass, which had just been filled. "Touché."

"Something we agree on, though he thinks he's still quite the ladies' man."

"Old ladies, perhaps," she replied with a smug look.

She took a sip of wine, and he did the same as he pondered his next topic. "How long are you in London?"

Smiling, she set the glass down. "Until my parents return from Paris. We have a townhouse there," she said. "I wasn't invited to accompany them, and I certainly didn't feel like spending my time in Scotland. My cousin obliged when asked by my father."

He shook his head. "I can't imagine a young woman like you not wanting to visit Paris."

"I never said I didn't want to visit Paris. My family lived in France for a time. I've been to Paris on many occasions. Right now, I find it boring."

"Perhaps you need to change your social acquaintances in Paris. Seek out those who are more suited to whatever it is you like to do."

She arched a brow and picked up her spoon. "Perhaps."

They ate their soup without another word. She was going to make sure they both had a miserable time. Why? He picked up his wineglass as the footman took away the first course and another brought broiled salmon with capers along with perch in cream sauce. He observed her wrinkling her nose, but pretended he hadn't seen. It was actually quite cute how she did that.

She turned away from him to answer a question her other dinner partner asked. Of all men to place her next to, the flamboyant Viscount Newton was the worst possible choice. Marriage had never stopped the viscount from shamelessly flirting with young, unattached women such as Lady Clare. Even the man's manner of dress was offensive. He looked like a peacock with all the colors he wore.

Parr took a forkful of the creamed fish and gazed down the table to where Clevedon sat. The two made eye contact, and the duke had the audacity to smile and raise his glass of wine in his direction. Smug bastard. He was having fun with this. Parr suddenly felt as though he was in the lion's den, and no one was going to rescue him. He shook his head. His other dinner partner was engaged in conversation with another, so he set his fork aside and downed his wine.

By the time the crisp-skinned roast duck was served, Parr was more than ready to leave. Lady Clare was still engaged in conversation with the peacock, and the lady to his left, Lady Hemsley, regrettably had little to say beyond remarking upon the weather or inquiring about his siblings.

Having lost his parents in a violent carriage accident, Wexford had been left with three sisters and two brothers living at home. After a reasonable mourning period, he sent Gregory and George off to Eton. His younger sisters, Violet and Jenny, would be ready for their coming out over the next two years. Perhaps they'd each find a suitable husband. Their older sister, Alexandria, certainly had. Hers had been an arranged marriage, the couple having met only two days prior to their wedding. Somehow, she and Viscount Sansbury had accepted their fate. In fact, now they seemed to adore each other. If it were a farce, they kept it well hidden, and since they were staying here in London with him, he was certain he would know if there were marital discord between the two.

"My cousin says you're quite the horseman," he heard Lady Clare say, bringing him out of his brooding and back to the dinner party.

"I enjoy riding as much as the next man."

"Come, my lord. Don't be so modest. I understand you ride a magnificent black stallion."

"Hercules is quite handsome. He has more stamina than any of my other horses," he replied.

Dessert would be served next, and if he were going to make a move and invite her for a walk or carriage ride, it would have to be soon. Once dinner was over, the ladies would retire to the drawing room for tea, and he would be locked in here to enjoy port, cigars, and politics with the men.

"Perhaps I'll see you riding him through the park."

Was she playing with him, or did she hope he would invite her to ride with him?

"Would you care to accompany me for a ride through the park? I could call on you tomorrow afternoon. I have a nice gray mare I think you'd find much to your liking."

She let the footman take her plate before replying, then looked Parr directly in the eyes. Hers were the darkest green he thought he'd ever seen. Like deep-hued emeralds.

"Regrettably, my lord, I must decline. Her Grace made previous arrangements for us to visit her modiste."

"Surely that won't take all day."

"It'll take most of the day. Perhaps another time?"

He wasn't sure if she were setting him up only to let him down again. He would take that chance.

"Yes, perhaps another time," he replied.

Parr was relieved when dessert was served. His friend's bride had made sure to serve almond cheesecake, one of his favorites. At least a piece of this delectable cake wouldn't unsettle him the way Lady Clare did.

Time came when dinner was over, and the gentlemen rose as the ladies quietly left the dining room. The peacock beat him to speaking with Lady Clare before they retired to the drawing room. Parr simply nodded in her direction. She met his nod with a smirk and quickly turned away from him.

He sat brooding through a lively discussion about some controversy in Parliament. He barely heard a word being said around him. Instead, he found he couldn't stop thinking about his dinner partner and how she'd deliberately set out to toy with him. One thing was certain, Clevedon was correct: his cousin did have a tart tongue. Problem was, he actually found it to be a breath of fresh air compared to the simpering demeanors of the usual ladies of the ton.

Lady Clare was quite pleasing in appearance. She'd make some lucky man a wonderful wife. Just not him. It was evident by the manner in which she spoke with him and the fact that she refused his offer of a ride in the park that she wasn't interested in him.

When the gentlemen rose to join the ladies, Parr glanced at his old friend. He needed to take his leave. Now.

"I take it my cousin was unkind?" Clevedon inquired.

"No, not at all. From the little time I spoke with her, I can see she's a complicated young woman."

"Yes, she is," he replied.

Parr finished off his port. "I need to go. Please pass on my thanks to your lovely bride for such a delightful evening."

"You can tell her yourself," Clevedon said. "You'll not give my cousin the satisfaction of thinking she's thwarted any so-called attempt to set her up with a respectable man."

"Really, I don't wish to have her humiliate me in front of your friends, and I fear that may be her next move."

"She won't," the duke replied as he poured them both another glass of port. "Her father sent her to me to find her a suitable match."

"I thought they went to Paris." He took the glass from Clevedon and swirled the dark amber liquid.

"They did. She's chased away every eligible man in Edinburgh. Her parents thought allowing her to stay here without them might be what she needs."

Parr drummed his fingers on the arm of the chair. "She seems quite intelligent. More than most."

"She is. Perhaps if you ask her to go on a carriage ride, you'd see that. You'd be surprised by the subjects she's interested in, many of which are not topics you'd normally converse with your dinner partner about."

"I already asked her, and she declined, politely, of course. Something about her and the duchess having previous plans to visit the duchess's modiste."

Clevedon nodded. "She is correct. I remember my wife mentioning something about acquiring ball gowns for the Duke of Liverpool's annual summer ball."

"Perhaps I need not press her."

The duke snorted. "Write her a note, send it with flowers in the morning. Tell her you'll call on her to accompany you on a carriage ride at three."

"I tried to suggest just such a thing."

"My wife told me the appointment was late morning. Send the flowers early enough."

Parr shook his head and downed the remaining port. "Do you really think she'll accept?"

"It would be rude not to. I'll also apprise my bride of your dilemma. She seems to have my cousin's ear."

"You're really sure about her?"

Clevedon smiled. "If I didn't think the two of you wouldn't be a perfect match, you wouldn't have been invited this evening. I'd have suggested someone else, when in fact the only person I can see as a match for her is you. It's time for you to move on, my friend."

He wasn't sure if he wanted Clevedon setting him up with his cousin. He was in mourning, or at least he told himself he was. Gentlemen officially mourned far less than women. They had to be able to go back to their businesses. His friend was right though, it was time he moved on. "Very well, I'll do as you suggest."

"Women love flowers. If you want to make a strong

impression on her, send her pink roses. A huge vase full of pink roses."

"Something to impress her. Trust me, by the time I arrive to collect her for our carriage drive, Lady Clare will be most impressed."

Clevedon smiled broadly and rose from his chair. "Knowing you I'm sure my cousin will be speechless. That's saying quite a bit, as Lady Clare is not often without an opinion."

"So I gather."

"You'll be fine. Trust me. Let's rejoin the others."

Parr arched a brow. "Very well. For a while, I suppose, but I can't stay long." Perhaps he should just trust Clevedon. Lady Clare might not like it if she thought she was being manipulated, but he was sure with his charm he could easily win her over.

Lady Clare awoke the next morning and dressed in a simple dark blue muslin day dress. She'd brought her lady's maid, Agnes, from Scotland. She barely heard whatever the older woman was going on about because she'd simply learned not to pay attention. Agnes had at one time been her mother's lady's maid. A misunderstanding had occurred between the two women, thus ending Agnes's position with her mother. Clare wasn't sure what had happened, exactly, but her mother quickly found the maid another position within the house as Clare's lady's maid.

She thought of the Earl of Wexford. He was more than pleasing to look at, with his blond hair that curled at the ends and which he wore tied back in a queue. His blue eyes were as dark as the waters of the Mediterranean, but they had a haunted appearance to them if one dared look closely enough. He had a square chin and high cheekbones. His nose was slightly off, making her wonder if it'd been broken in a fight, yet it lent him an air of indefinable masculinity.

His tall stature ensured he had a most commanding presence.

She smiled, remembering being seated next to him at dinner. She'd done her best to appear aloof, though she'd kept her tongue in check as her cousin asked. She wasn't going to fall into the arms of the first gentleman who paid her attention while she was in London. Clare knew her parents had left her behind because they hoped her cousin might know of a peer willing to marry her.

Then Wexford had to ask her to join him for a carriage ride through the park. She had to refuse, no matter how much she'd wanted to accept or wanted him to show her his horses. Being that Parr was the first of many suitors with whom she'd need to contend with it was easy enough to nip this in the bud. When her cousin asked her what had transpired between them, she could tell him she thought she and the earl would be ill-suited. That would take care of that.

Regardless, she felt bad for using the man. He had been a decent enough dinner companion, at least when she wasn't ignoring him by paying attention to the gentleman seated to her right. That one had been annoying.

"My gloves and reticule, please, Agnes. Then I'm off to shop with Her Grace. Be sure the pale green gown is ready for this evening."

The maid handed the items to Clare with a smile. "That gown is one of my favorites, milady."

Clare nodded and left the room. As she neared the bottom of the stairs, she noted a large vase of pink roses in two shades sitting on a table in the middle of the entrance hall. Their beauty almost took her breath away. Never had she seen the two hues combined like this, and there had to be at least three dozen blooms.

"These came for you a while ago. There's a card on the table," the duchess said, entering from the drawing room door.

"For me? Who would be sending me such gorgeous roses?" She smiled and opened the card.

"Who are they from?"

She tried to hide her disappointment. She had been hoping they were from someone else. "The Earl of Wexford. He's going to call this afternoon. He wishes to take me for a drive."

"You shouldn't look so crestfallen. The earl keeps his feelings close to his heart, or at least that's what my husband tells me. Especially since his wife died. You should be happy, Clare, that Wexford may be interested."

"I am," she lied. "They were simply unexpected, that's all." She leaned over and inhaled the fragrance while trying to control her true feelings.

"If you're ready, we should be on our way," Her Grace said.

Clare smiled. "Come, let's go indulge ourselves, shall we?"

The sights and sounds of London passed them by as the carriage made its way through the heavy traffic. Clare wasn't paying attention as she knew she should be. If she were going to find Francois, she knew she'd have to sneak out of the house, or when the duke and duchess had business elsewhere together. She'd sent word to his last known place of residence as soon as she'd arrived, but had not heard back from him. This meant one of two things: either Francois had moved on, or he didn't want her any longer. Or her cousin had intercepted her letters.

She had met Francois Bernas three years ago on a family holiday to France. They were staying at a chateau her father had rented for the summer. Francois's father was a merchant and had business dealings with her father. His father brought him along as his apprentice. Though it was an impossible, complicated friendship, the two became lovestruck.

Once her father realized what was going on, having been told by Mr. Bernas himself, the duke sent his headstrong daughter back to Scotland, forbidding any further correspondence with the young man. The pair still managed to write each other. His father had been equally as unforgiving as her own. He sent his disgraced son to stay with relatives in the north of France.

Francois had managed to put aside money and fled his relations for London. He vowed his love to her and promised the two of them would start anew in America. All they had to do was find each other and flee.

Interestingly enough, her cousin had married an American and was more than happy to share details of her life in the new country with Clare. Clare had feigned an interest in America, hoping to figure where Francois may have gone. So far, she had no clear answers. He simply had to be in London still, working to have enough money for passage and a new life. She would find him, of that she was sure.

The earl might be a more valuable ally than she first realized. Surely he knew London well. If she accepted his offer to show her around London, she might be able to find Francois. Perhaps this afternoon, she would innocently ask him about the area of London where Francois had last been living. If her cousin had indeed had her correspondence intercepted, then Francois could still be residing at the address she had.

WEXFORD ARRIVED BACK AT CLEVEDON'S HOME THE following afternoon to fulfill his invitation to Lady Clare. Though he'd met her only the night before, he found himself drawn to her. She wasn't the demure, quiet young woman one usually found in the ballrooms, each looking for a well-to-do husband. No, Lady Clare had a fire about her that appealed to him.

He was waiting for her in the grand hall, admiring the roses he'd had delivered, when Clevedon strode in.

"Wexford, Lady Clare will be a few minutes. While you're waiting, why don't we go to my study for a chat."

"Sounds ominous."

Clevedon chuckled and led the way. As they entered, he motioned Wexford to a leather chair in front of his desk while he poured two glasses of whiskey.

"I needed to speak with you," Clevedon started.

"About Lady Clare?"

He nodded. "Yes. Please, don't misunderstand me. I don't wish you to spy on her, I simply need to know if she asks questions a woman wouldn't normally ask, such as how to get to certain parts of London."

Wexford accepted the glass and took a contemplative swallow. "May I ask why?"

"Of course. It seems there's a young man here in London for whom she is searching. She met the boy in France. One of those unfortunate incidents where a young high-bred woman meets and falls in love with an improper, untitled gentleman. I have it on good authority the young man is indeed here in Town."

"That explains a great deal, actually," Wexford replied thoughtfully.

"I've been intercepting correspondence that she has

been sending the young man. Apparently, they intended to flee to America."

Wexford cocked a brow. "And he's unacceptable to her father?"

"Very. He's the son of a merchant with whom the duke works. His father banished him to Northern France, but apparently, the two have been corresponding anyway. He's here in London, and in the meantime, I have a man following him to discover where he lives and if he works. Moving to America would require money."

"Yes, it would," Wexford replied and finished his whiskey. "I'll keep an eye on her. I'm sure she'll slip up."

"Depends. She's an intelligent woman."

"I am surprised the duke didn't arranged a marriage for her. That would be a certain way to ensure she forgot about this young man."

"He's looking for a suitable prospect. He'd rather not force her into an arranged marriage."

Wexford studied his friend for a moment. "And that's why you're trying to find a man with whom she might strike a spark?"

"A man such as you, my friend." The duke smiled.

Wexford felt a bit cornered. "It's too soon. I'm still in mourning."

Clevedon shook his head. "Think it over. In the meantime, I'm sure Clare will try to sneak her questions in, thinking you won't be aware of what's going on."

He rose and set down his glass. "I will, but it's likely moot as the lady seems reluctant to spend time with me. However, I don't mind doing you this favor and shall report back with any information I can glean from her."

"Thank you. Now you best get back to the hall. I'm sure

my cousin is looking everywhere for you, and she hates to be kept waiting."

"I'll keep that in mind."

He walked back to the grand hall and found Lady Clare pacing the floor. She indeed did not look amused.

"I apologize. Clevedon had a matter requiring both our attention."

She raised an imperious brow and lifted her chin. "Don't bother apologizing. It doesn't become you. I know that my cousin, being a duke, believes the world revolves around him. My father is the same way. You were merely doing his bidding."

Wexford bit back a laugh. Lady Clare was most observant, but also rebellious when it came to the aristocracy. She stretched every rule written or unwritten. It made him wonder if it might perhaps be because of this Frenchman she was supposedly in love with.

"If you're ready?" He took his hat from the nearby butler and placed it neatly onto his head.

"Yes, let's go. I need to be free of my prison for a few hours."

He shook his head as he followed her out of the house. As he helped her into his phaeton, he couldn't help but notice how the sun shone off her glorious copper-red hair.

"I thought we might go to the park." He settled beside her and gathered the pair's reins. "Your cousin's man and your lady's maid will follow us."

"I'd rather see some of the sights the town has to offer. The park is the socially acceptable place to take me, but I wish to see something different."

"But..."

"Do you know where Simmons Street is? Take me there."

He shook his head. "Absolutely not. Simmons is near the docks and in a very dangerous neighborhood. Why on earth would you want to go there?"

"A friend told me about it, and you must be mistaken. It couldn't be anywhere near the docks."

He fisted the reins and set them in his lap, turning to face her. "No, it is near the docks, and I will not take you there. It is your friend who is mistaken."

She began to pout, but evidently thought better of it. Wexford braced for her wrath. She was clearly a spoiled brat and used to getting her own way.

"Lord Wexford, you do know who my father is. My cousin as well. I'm sure I could make your life miserable if I so chose. A mere mention to either of them will put you in your place."

Wexford turned his eyes to the traffic in front of him, knowing he might burst out laughing if he even looked at her. "Yes, your father and cousin are two very powerful dukes. Your cousin is also a dear friend of mine. Do you really think I wasn't forewarned of your spoiled ways?" he said. "I'm surprised your father hasn't arranged a marriage for you."

"He wouldn't dare."

"Perhaps, but again, I understand your dowry to be one of the largest in all Great Britain. Why wouldn't he try to arrange a match?"

"He's tried and failed. Now take me to Simmons Street. I command you."

He barked a laugh. In front of her this time. "You command me? Lady Clare, I'm not one of your servants you can order about. You'd best remember that. We will not be going anywhere near Simmons Street."

She slumped back in her seat, obviously disappointed.

Her plump bottom lip protruded. She was pouting. Lady Clare wasn't used to not getting her way.

With a shake of his head, Wexford maneuvered the carriage into the park and found a place where he could pull to the side. If he wanted to help Clevedon, he needed to win her over. Wait! Did he really want to do that? Whatever or whoever was on Simmons Street was important to her. The young Frenchman, he'd bet. Perhaps if he made her an offer...

"Lady Clare, I'm sorry you're upset with me for not taking you where you asked, but as I told you, it's simply not a safe place for a high-born lady such as yourself. Your cousin would never forgive me if anything happened to you."

She flashed her dark green eyes at him, then turned away as though she was thinking of how to answer him without being harsh.

"If you tell me the address and whom it is you're looking for, I'll do it for you."

She turned her head, and her eyes narrowed slyly. "Why?"

"Because the docks..."

"Yes, yes, I know. The docks are not a safe place for women like me," she interrupted.

"They're not safe for any woman."

She cocked her head and sat up a bit straighter. "Why would you want to do this for me? What's in it for you?"

"I want nothing in return, I assure you. I simply wish to help you out. If this person you seek is still living there, I could arrange a meeting."

Her eyes brightened. "You'd do that?"

He nodded. "Yes, I would."

"How do I know you won't return to Clevedon and tell

him everything? He'd lock me in my room for the remainder of my time in London."

She wasn't going to make this easy, but Wexford had anticipated she was going to be difficult. He shrugged. "You're going to have to trust me on this."

"Very well, I'll accept your generous offer. Just remember, you've offered to do this without anything expected in return."

"I accept," he replied.

She poured out the entire story of the young man she'd fallen in love with in France, how her father and his had conspired to send each of them away, refusing to allow the friendship to continue. The pair had obviously made some pact to meet up in London. Her plans, she said, were uncertain. Was she lying or telling the truth?

Wexford paid close attention, watching her every move, the way her eyes sparkled when she spoke of her young paramour, the way her delicate hands fluttered, then closed when she described the fathers convening to keep them apart. "I'll go there first thing in the morning. I'll call on you late morning and offer to take you riding in the park."

She gave him a brilliant smile that quite made his breath catch. "Thank you, my lord."

He picked up the reins to guide his team of high-stepping bays back out into the heavy traffic in the park. "You're welcome. I pray I return with the answers you anticipate."

"I'm sure you will."

The conversation about her Frenchman ended, and instead, she turned to asking him questions about the park. She seemed truly interested in the history of the area, or at least that was the façade she was allowing him to see.

"How did you come to be so interested in English history?" he asked.

A hint of a smile appeared on her lovely lips. "It's always been intertwined with Scottish history, you know."

"Sometimes not in good ways."

"I'm afraid you're right, my lord."

"Would you like to stop and walk for a while?"

"No, I'm enjoying this much better. Another time."

He nodded, unsurprised by her reply. "Another time."

"Could I ask you a personal question, my lord?"

She had his curiosity. He arched a brow. "Ask away."

"Why aren't you betrothed or married? You're certainly well thought of, educated, and handsome enough."

He pondered how to answer, and how detailed his answer should be. Finally, he said, "I am a widower. My wife died in a senseless accident involving my phaeton about a year ago. Therefore, I have no interest in a marriage at this time."

"My condolences on the loss of your wife. Are you sure you're not at least looking for another?"

"No."

She peered at him with that probing, intelligent gaze. "And why is that?"

"I'm not ready. Besides, I haven't met anyone suitable even if I were. I don't wish for a young, innocent debutant as my bride. I require someone more worldly."

"Yes, I can understand. There's only so far conversation about the weather can go."

"Exactly." He chuckled. "I can't imagine you ever being at a loss for words or giggling at any inane topic."

She flashed him a warm smile. "I never have, my lord."

"Then that makes you a very rare bloom indeed."

She didn't blush, but instead turned the conversation to him once more. "I understand your family seat is located in West Sussex."

"It is. Wexford Castle is exactly that. A castle."

"And is it as cold and drafty as the ones in Scotland?"

"It is, though I will admit to having had certain aspects of it updated."

His eye caught on a few people he knew. No one he wanted to stop and introduce Lady Clare to at the moment, however. He wanted this first outing to be theirs alone, especially since she was beginning to let him see another side of herself. He kept the phaeton rolling and simply acknowledged them with a passing nod.

"What of siblings?" she pressed.

"I have many. A sister who is older, then four who are younger. And you?"

"Only my brother, Charles, but he's in the spice trade and in India."

"India? That's the other side of the world."

She nodded. "Yes. My father doesn't approve of his decision either. He believes Charles should be preparing himself to run the dukedom's estates. That sort of thing."

"I'm sure he'll come around. Sometimes a young man needs one grand adventure before he settles."

"I'm sure you're right, my lord, though I'm not certain how my parents are going to take to the news that his bride is of Indian descent."

Wexford quickly closed his mouth. She'd shared a secret with him. "He's married, in secret? How is it you know?"

"Duncan made me promise not to tell our parents. When he comes home, he'll present her to the family."

"Seems you're not the only one in your family who has secrets."

"Yes, you're right, of course. I suppose we're both rebellious in that regard."

He smiled. "Nothing wrong with that, and I'm sure your parents will come to accept your brother's choice in a wife."

"But you don't think they will approve of my choice. Nor do you. Am I correct, my lord?"

"If that's the choice you make, I'm sure eventually they will come to accept him once they see how happy he makes you," he replied. "My feelings on the matter are of no consequence."

She glanced aside, looking out at couples walking along a well-manicured pathway. "Of course they're not," she choked out. For a quick moment, Wexford thought he saw tears pooling at the corners of her eyes.

"I didn't mean to upset you."

She shook her head and dabbed her lashes with her gloved fingers. "You didn't. I find myself in unusual circumstances."

He nodded. He hoped he hadn't ruined their afternoon by mentioning this young man. He would honor his word and find out for her if the young man was still living at the address. He always kept his word. Something about the entire situation niggled at him. And something else was bothering him even more than looking in on her young paramour. Could he possibly be opening his cold heart to her? And was she, despite the wall she'd placed around her heart, also thawing toward him?

3

Wexford found himself more confused than ever by the time he returned home late that afternoon. Spending the afternoon with Lady Clare had released a whirlwind of emotions. Emotions he hadn't allowed out of the locked box within his heart since Matilda had died so suddenly.

She kept him engaged and intrigued, unlike any other young woman he'd been introduced to since coming out of mourning. In spite of her sometimes acerbic tongue, he found her witty candor refreshing. He could talk to her about a vast range of topics. She never giggled or did any of the other silly things debutants often did.

He would find out about this young Frenchman, not only for Clevedon's sake, but for Lady Clare's as well. But if the young man was indeed living near the docks, did he want to risk her safety by letting her know his findings? Would she rush to the young man's side, would she try once again to slip a message to him, or would the young man have fled already?

Wexford sent a man down to Simmons Street to see

whether this young man was indeed living there or if he'd moved on. If his man found the Frenchman had departed, Wexford instructed him to make discreet inquiries.

He walked into the comfortable sitting room in his town-home, poured himself a glass of whiskey, then stood by the fire, contemplating his next move.

As he had no social engagements this evening, he'd decided to have dinner at White's. That would be much easier than having his cook prepare a dinner for one, and he wouldn't be left alone with his thoughts. He'd spent far too many nights looking into the bottom of a bottle of whiskey in an attempt to allay his guilt over the death of his wife.

If only he'd stopped her that fateful afternoon, she might still be alive. She'd goaded him into letting her drive a new phaeton he had just that day taken possession of. Matilda had been drinking, as she did most days, starting early in the afternoon.

Rather than take the phaeton around to the stables, he'd parked it outside the front door of his country home, wanting to show it off to his wife by taking her for a quick drive. But when she first spotted the vehicle, she became belligerent because she wanted to try it out. After finally allowing him to assist her into the vehicle, she picked up the reins, let off the brake, and goaded the pair of high-spirited mares into a frenzy. The rest was a nightmare of the worst making. Her abuse of the carriage horses had been abominable. Her drinking had become a daily ritual. She was unpredictable, going from one emotion to another in the blink of an eye. And yet he had loved her, or he thought he had, which was why he tolerated her behavior.

Since that fateful day, Wexford spoke neither of her nor the accident. If someone inquired or gave their condolences, his responses were short and clipped.

After that, he spent the better part of three months drunk and unkempt, rarely tending to business matters or leaving his estate. He was mourning the death of his young wife, and he took advantage of the situation.

That was until Clevedon and Littleton, Marquess of Dover, intervened. Both were friends from their days at Eton who checked in on him on a regular basis. They'd left instructions with his valet and butler to send word if matters got worse. When word reached them of his dissolution, both flew to Wexford's side to help sober him up and bring him back to the land of the living.

Now, Wexford found himself in a similar situation. Already, he was having feelings for Clevedon's cousin, Lady Clare. He must find out about her young Frenchman and nothing more. His heart simply wouldn't survive being broken again, and he knew he couldn't return to that dark place.

So to keep his thoughts from drifting to the past, he would simply head upstairs, bathe, dress, and head to White's for an evening out. Hopefully, one or more of his friends who were unattached might be there, or else he would simply enjoy a good steak and afterward, a brandy and cigar before returning home.

Tomorrow, his sister, Alexandria, was due to visit, though Wexford truly thought she was there to check in on him before she and her husband departed for the Continent. His other siblings were either visiting their aunt Beth in Brighton or, in the case of the twins, George and Gregory, were off visiting their mother's uncle Thomas for a month. Alexandria had agreed with him when he presented his proposal of what to do with their brothers and sisters. At least for a while.

Wexford downed his glass of whiskey, refilled it, and

climbed the stairs to his chambers to bathe and change. Tonight was his, because tomorrow, his solitude would be intruded upon, and hopefully his man would find some sign of this Francois Bernas.

Even if he found the young man, a match with Lady Clare was still out of the question. Her father wouldn't allow her to marry a commoner, and Clevedon would honor his uncle's wishes. Clevedon was going to have his hands full with his cousin if Bernas was found. Lady Clare was a spirited young woman, and not one to necessarily do as she was told. If she put her mind to it, Wexford felt sure she would disappear with the young man, and he wasn't about to let that happen. She was pulling hard on his heartstrings. So hard, Wexford found himself unnerved.

THOUGHTS OF THE EARL OF WEXFORD HAD CONSUMED FAR too much of her time. Clare was uncomfortable with how this handsome, titled English gentleman occupied her mind. Today, he'd let his guard down and told her about his late wife and her tragic accident, not in great detail, but the man had shared what was clearly a sensitive memory with her.

She wondered why her cousin hadn't mentioned it to her. Clevedon's wife, Savannah, hadn't even mentioned Lord Wexford was widowed. Looking back, Clare assumed everyone was protecting him from having to discuss the matter. He'd only recently come out of mourning and resumed his life. What was it about his late wife that kept Wexford in the protective circle of those closest to him?

She'd heard no gossip at the balls and soirees she'd

attended thus far. Even most of the mothers respected him, not pushing their young daughters in front of him.

He was a handsome man who cut a dashing figure. He would make any woman a fine husband, but right now wasn't the time. His heart was still healing.

Which led her to another oddity: why was he so interested in inquiring about Francois? Was he acting on her cousin's behalf or did he truly see how much she loved Francois and was sincere in his offer to help her find him?

"Clare?"

She found Her Grace watching her, an amused smile on her lips. How long had Savannah sat here in the drawing room thinking about her afternoon?

"I apologize. My mind was elsewhere, I'm afraid."

"So I can see. It wouldn't have anything to do with Lord Wexford, would it?" Savannah stirred a cup of tea she'd just poured herself.

Instinctively, Clare picked up her own cup and observed her cousin-in-law over the rim. "In a manner of speaking, yes."

"He was a gentleman, wasn't he? No, of course he was. Wexford is always a proper gentleman."

Clare worked on an embroidery piece. Clevedon had excused himself after dinner, citing a business meeting in the morning for which he needed to prepare.

"He spoke briefly about the loss of his wife. Matilda, I believe was her name?"

"He did?"

"He told me she died in a freak accident involving a phaeton."

Savannah nodded. "Yes, she did. She was reckless at times. If Wexford told her no, she would forge ahead nevertheless. I believe he blames himself in part for the accident, as he'd just purchased the vehicle."

"That doesn't surprise me, from what I know of him," Clare said, then paused, biting her lip. "Did he love her?"

"He was devastated by her death."

Clare shook her head. "You're avoiding my question."

"Because it's not something I should be discussing with you. The details should come from Wexford and not me. It's his place to decide what he feels comfortable sharing with the world. I'll leave it at that."

"Is that why you and my cousin have been pushing us together? He needs to begin to socialize, and I need to find a suitable husband?"

Savannah smiled demurely. "I will admit, Clevedon thought you would be someone Wexford might be interested in. You're everything Matilda never was." Clare was as headstrong as Matilda had been, but that's where the similarities ended.

"I don't even want to know what that means," Clare replied. "I still have no interest in any man, especially if they're chosen for me. My heart knows what it wants, and when the right man comes along, I will know."

"Very well," the duchess murmured.

Clare changed the subject. "So tell me about the Duke and Duchess of Liverpool's ball. You've said an invitation is highly coveted."

"It is. Everyone who's anyone will be there."

"So I understand."

"The ball is quite extravagant, from what I understand. This will be my first as well."

Clare smiled. "Are you terrified? I ask only because America cannot compete as they have no peerage."

"True, though my American friends and family might disagree with you."

"I'm sure. Have you and Clevedon given any thought about hosting your own ball?"

She smiled again. "He mentioned it. I was hoping our first such party could be held at our estate in Scotland."

"The dowager could be of great assistance. She loves extravagant parties, and from what I understand from my mother, her and Clevedon's soirees would rival any held in London."

"That's good to know," she replied. "Clevedon has alluded to the fact that his mother would be a huge asset in helping me plan for a ball on such a grand scale."

"Your dinner party was a smashing success, you know."

"True, though I'm sure most of our guests were more curious about the duke's American wife." She threaded a needle, close to finishing off the delicate pattern.

Clare laughed subtly. "Then use it to your advantage."

Her cousin's bride might well be her ally. She seemed to side with women who were different, such as herself. The duchess was American and looked upon as an oddity by the ton. Perhaps, once she found out what Wexford discovered-about Francois, she could take the duchess into her confidence.

"May I ask you something personal," the duchess inquired.

"Of course." *Here it comes, she's about to inquire of my affections for someone common like Francois.*

"If you find your young Frenchman, what are you plans? What sort of life could the two of you have?"

"I don't know. Francois came here to find employment in order to put aside enough money for us to marry and start anew elsewhere. Though my life would be nothing like it is now, I am certain I could adjust to anything."

"I only ask because you know your father will never give him your dowry. That's part of the reason the duke is so against any sort of relationship. He believes the young man is after your dowry."

"Yes, my father has made that abundantly clear. Francois and I may not have much, but we'll have each other."

The duchess smiled. "Spoken like a true romantic."

4

F rancois Bernas, the young man with whom Lady Clare was infatuated, had boarded a ship bound for America a week before. Headed for New York, to be exact. Though Wexford sighed with relief, he knew this information would devastate her.

He met Clevedon at White's, not wanting to share what he'd learned in the duke's home. He didn't want to risk Lady Clare overhearing. He would inform her later when he called on her. He planned to take her to the park again, this time on horseback. Clevedon had assured him his cousin was an accomplished rider. He'd picked out a gray mare as a test to see what skills she possessed. Perhaps it would distract her from thoughts of Bernas.

Clevedon sat down in a well-worn leather chair inside White's and signaled for a footman to bring him a whiskey. "What have you learned?" he asked Parr.

"Mr. Bernas boarded a ship bound for New York about a week ago," Parr murmured. "That explains why there have been no letters from him."

"Do you imagine he never intended to take Lady Clare,

or do you think he'll send for her once he's settled?" Parr asked.

The duke accepted a crystal glass from the footman and sat back. "None of his correspondence made mention of sending for her. My thought on the matter is that once he found out her father was not going to give him her dowry, he made plans to travel to America alone. He'll never send for her."

"I agree," Wexford replied. "Once correspondence ceased, his plans became obvious."

"She's going to be devastated. I dread telling her what I've discovered."

Wexford swallowed the last of his whiskey. "Let me. I'm taking her riding in the park this afternoon. It'll be easier if I tell her. If you do, she might not be so forgiving."

"I don't see why."

"She begged me to take her in search of him. I refused, explaining the docks were no place for a lady like her. I may have mentioned I would look into the matter."

Clevedon cocked a brow. "I see, and you're right. It would be gentler if it came from you. She sees me as an extension of her father at the moment."

"Perhaps once she's had a week or so, she'll be receptive to a more suitable match."

"And are you including yourself when you say a more suitable match?" The duke smiled.

"I don't know. I find my feelings run amok around her."

"Don't deny yourself happiness, Wexford. Matilda is gone, and there's nothing you can do to change that. If you think you might have an interest in courting my cousin, you have my permission."

"Still, I feel as though I'm being unfaithful."

Clevedon finished his whiskey and caught the eye of the

footman to see if their table was ready. "If it were Matilda sitting here, she wouldn't hesitate to move on," he replied. "Now come, let's see about having some lunch. You'll need all your strength when you ride with my young cousin."

Wexford knew in his heart his friend was right. Matilda had been fickle and had always done whatever might help her rise in status. Once, right after they married, she made it known that she could have done better than a mere earl. It mattered not how much money he had. She was lavish in her spending from the very start, and nothing he said brought her under control.

Not until he arranged an allowance for her and that became the only money she had for her fripperies. It was then that she began taunting him about his rank, just as she had the day she died.

"You wouldn't have an issue with me courting her?" he asked, putting thoughts of Matilda aside.

"I think you are one of few men who could tame her, if Clare even can be tamed. I've watched her with you. Since your initial meeting, her demeanor toward you has changed. She no longer speaks with such an acid tongue to you. She seems relaxed in your company," Clevedon said.

"That may all change this afternoon, I'm afraid," Wexford murmured.

"As I said, give her time to grasp that her Frenchman has abandoned her without a word." Clevedon added, "You must make no mention of this to Clare, but Bernas came to call on her right after she arrived, if you can believe that. He was informed she would not be receiving him, and told to leave immediately."

Wexford nodded. "That took a lot of nerve, showing up at your home unannounced."

"Indeed."

"Did your man send him away, or did you meet with him?"

"I happened to be walking to my study when I heard him demanding to see my cousin. It was I who told him he wasn't welcome and that Clare would not ever be receiving him."

Before Wexford could reply, an older man approached them. "If you are ready, a dining room has become available, Your Grace."

Clevedon nodded to the man and rose from his chair. He peered at Wexford. "Shall we?"

"Yes. I must admit, I'm hungrier than I thought."

The pair followed the man to a private dining room with burgundy-hued wallpaper with gold accents. A table was set up for them to one side. They sat, and a footman poured them each a glass of red wine.

"Steak all right with you?" Clevedon asked.

"Absolutely."

"Two steaks, rare."

The footman bowed before turning to leave the room.

When they were alone, Clevedon took a long swallow of wine. "I trust you're going to the Duke of Liverpool's ball?"

"I hadn't planned on it, but I did receive an invitation, and Lady Clare mentioned she was accompanying you and the duchess."

"Good. Reply to the invitation," he said. "Be prepared. I expect a line of men wanting to sign her dance card once she arrives."

"Not much I can do about that beyond requesting one or two dances." The absurdity of polite society grated on him sometimes.

"Make sure one is the supper set."

Wexford snorted as he picked up his wineglass. "Pray tell how I can make that happen with all the men lined up?"

"My wife is going to make the suggestion to my cousin to leave two spots open for you."

"I keep liking your duchess more and more, Clevedon."

Clevedon smiled briefly. "I wouldn't exactly call her devious, but she's determined to distract my cousin's attentions."

A few minutes later, their meal arrived. They discussed politics and horses while they dined. Once they finished, port was brought to them. It was an aged Portuguese port Wexford had sampled once before. He preferred good whiskey to port, but this was aged perfectly and went down smoothly.

"Speaking of your cousin, I need to depart. She will be waiting."

"Yes, and don't be late."

"Which is why I'm leaving now."

"I'll be interested to learn of her response to the news."

They parted at the door, each going their separate ways. Wexford headed to the mews where he stabled his horses while in London. There he found a stable boy giving his stallion a final brushing.

He thanked the young boy and led both his stallion and the mare he'd selected for Lady Clare outside. He handed the reins to the mare to the stable boy while he mounted and gathered the stallion's reins. The black was eager for a run, and there were a couple of places in the park where they could do just that. He took the reins of the mare and made his way the four blocks to Clevedon's London home.

Wexford stopped in front of the brick home, which rose three stories from the street. A black iron fence enclosed the house, making it quite a stunning structure. A stable boy came out of nowhere to take the horses, then the front door opened, and Lady Clare rushed out.

He dismounted and handed the reins to the stable boy so that he might help Lady Clare mount the mare. He suppressed a smile when she frowned at the sight of the side saddle.

"In the future, Lord Wexford, I don't require a side saddle. I detest them and find they impede my riding abilities."

This time, he did smile. "I'll keep that in mind for the next time we ride."

"Make sure you do," she said tartly. For a second, he was afraid the old, acid-tongued Clare had returned.

"If you're ready," he said, "why don't we get started."

"Yes, let's. It's been a while since I've ridden."

"Really? I would have thought your father, and certainly Clevedon would have let you ride."

"Clevedon wanted to accompany me the first time I rode in the park. That's all well and good, but he's been busy since we arrived."

"Then I take it I'll make an acceptable substitute for your cousin?"

Her dark green eyes sparkled with mischief. "A far better substitute, my lord."

"Then let's go. The horses are anxious for some exercise."

They walked beside each other, and when they arrived at the park, Wexford led her to one of the horse paths. There were a number of riders, mainly gentlemen riding their fine horses. They were there to be seen as they acknowledged and spoke with peers or young ladies out for a stroll.

"Can we go for a good gallop?"

Wexford shook his head. "Not here. There's a section coming up where there should be less traffic. We can gallop them there. Just remember there might be fewer horses and people, and some don't adhere to rules of the park, as it were."

"Rules of the park? Are you kidding?"

"I never joke about such matters. Some men do whatever they like without regard to others."

"Yes, of course," she replied. "You must forgive me. It's been quite a while since I've ridden in a park."

"There's nothing to apologize for."

Several gentlemen tipped their hats to them, some of the men's gazes taking in Lady Clare. She did look stunning in her hunter-green riding outfit. But then anything would look good on this beauty. The sight of other men paying her attention sent a twinge of jealousy through him.

Finally, they cantered for a good while, stopping near a rather large pond. Wexford knew he now needed to have the conversation he'd been dreading. He was surprised she hadn't pounced on him the moment they entered the park.

He turned to face her. "I'm afraid I have news of your young man."

"What have you learned?" she asked. "From the look on your face, it can't be good."

"I'm afraid not. It seems he's left London for America."

She clearly fought to keep her eyes from tearing up, but she was losing. "I won't ask you for any details. It's over, then. I'm sure I won't be hearing from him again."

"Perhaps, once he's settled somewhere."

She sat up, her back ramrod straight. "Don't patronize me, my lord. He would have been in touch if he truly wanted me to know he was leaving. He would have told me he'd send for me later, but he didn't."

"I'm sorry."

"Don't be. I should have never been so foolish as to think he hadn't come to London with alternative plans which didn't include me."

He took one of her gloved hands in his. "Lady Clare, you're not foolish, and you will come out of this for the better."

"I am most grateful for your confidence in my abilities, my lord."

"Wexford. Please call me Wexford."

She blinked back tears. "Very well, Wexford. You may call me Clare if you wish, but only when we're alone," she replied. "May I be so bold as to ask what your given name is?"

"I'm known only as Wexford, or Parr by a few select individuals. My given name is horrid."

"A family name?"

He smiled. "Yes, dating back to the first earl."

"What does your family call you?"

"Wexford or Parr."

"If it's not too painful, may I inquire as to what Matilda called you?"

His eyes were cast down. "Wexford, unless she was angry, and then she called me by my given name, Milford."

She brightened. "Very well, Parr or Wexford it is, then."

He nodded. "Would you care to ride some more?"

"I would. This mare is lovely. She has a soft mouth and an easy canter. This has been a wonderful diversion. Thank you."

His lips twitched as he tried to hold back a smile. "I'm happy to be of assistance."

THE EARL WOULDN'T HAVE BEEN HER FIRST CHOICE FOR A husband, but now that she was getting to know him better, she was eager to learn more. Her cousin had told her Wexford kept his relationship with Lady Matilda to himself. Today had been the first time she'd been bold enough to inquire into his personal world by daring to ask him what his late wife called him. Surprisingly, he'd told her.

Francois had proven to be a disappointment, leaving England without so much as a brief note. Wexford was right about this, and though right now she felt her heart had been ripped from her chest, Clare knew she would continue on.

She was also smart enough to know that her father was planning on marrying her off. She would never allow that to happen. She would never be in a loveless marriage, made possible because of her sizeable dowry.

Wexford was looking more appealing each time she met him. He had done her a great service finding out what had become of Francois. Through his own tragedy, he'd stepped forward to offer her some closure to an impossible situation. Perhaps the earl was worthy of her attention.

The horse he'd brought for her to ride today was spectacular, a joy to ride. And when they'd had the discussion regarding side saddles, the earl—Parr—never treated her as an object with no mind of her own. He listened when she spoke, something rare among men of noble birth. Most thought women should stay at home or make them look good at public events, have an heir or two, and never, ever question their husband. Most importantly, she must have a sizeable dowry.

But that was when a man was pursuing a woman for a wife, and she wasn't sure Wexford was after a wife. In fact, she thought him to be undecided in the matter. Perhaps it was because his own wounds were still raw.

The Duke and Duchess of Liverpool's ball was coming up. It was a large affair, she'd been told, and she could use the night to review her choices. She hoped Wexford would be at the top of her list before the evening was over.

He interrupted her musings when he gestured toward a couple approaching them. "The Viscount and Viscountess of Hertford are right ahead. She will want to stop and talk."

"Why?"

He smiled wickedly. "Because she believes her younger sister, Lady Henrietta, would be perfect as my bride."

"And would she?" Clare inquired.

He leaned over to whisper, "I've never even met the chit."

"Oh my."

"Yes, I'm afraid it's rather embarrassing how my friends are lining up their relations, trying to get me to choose."

"Then don't choose. Not until you're ready."

As predicted, the viscount and his wife stopped to one side and beckoned them over. Introductions were made, and Clare felt herself being scrutinized by the viscountess.

"A Scotswoman. How fascinating," the viscountess trilled. The look on the woman's face told Clare she was anything but fascinated.

"Lady Clare is a cousin of Clevedon. She's visiting while her parents are on the continent," Wexford explained.

The woman arched a brow at the use of the duke's name. "I see. Are you enjoying your stay in London, Lady Clare?"

"Yes, I am. Wexford has been a dear to take me out riding and show me the sights."

Apparently sensing his wife's disapproval, the viscount

joined in. "Will you be attending the Duke of Liverpool's ball?"

Uncertain to whom the viscount was directing his question, Clare quickly responded. "Yes, I'll be attending with Clevedon and the duchess."

"Ah yes, the American duchess. I haven't had the pleasure," Viscountess Hertford replied. She turned shrewd brown eyes back to Wexford. "What about you, Lord Wexford? Will you be attending? My sister, Lady Henrietta, will be there as well."

"I plan to attend, my lady."

"Excellent. I trust you'll sign Lady Henrietta's dance card?"

"I'm sure I'll sign many dance cards that evening," Wexford replied graciously.

A few awkward moments later, Hertford and his wife departed, the viscountess's narrowed eyes watching Clare closely. She was obviously not liking what she saw, and Clare knew she viewed her as unwanted competition for her sister.

"You better watch yourself, Parr. Lady Hertford has eyes on you for her sister, and she doesn't appear to be a lady who takes a refusal well."

"Then Lady Hertford will need to learn to be quite disappointed," he said lowly.

"She certainly will," Clare agreed.

"Let's do something a little different. Don't let anyone sign your dance card for the supper set. I would very much like to dance with you then." He tipped his head, waiting for her answer.

"I'll be sure to pencil you in for two dances, my lord."

"I look forward to them."

She granted him a smile. "As do I, Parr."

Her heart should be exploding with grief at the news he'd brought her concerning Francois, but it wasn't. Had she not loved him as she once thought she had? Or had it been a case of simple infatuation, a means to get even with her father? Whatever the case, she felt herself drawn to the handsome man riding beside her.

She studied him for a moment as they rode along the path, his blond hair tousled from their vigorous gallops. He obviously enjoyed the outdoors, because his coloring was darker than most men. He was a faint bronze from his hours in the sun, riding or taking care of estate matters.

Her body betrayed her as goose flesh appeared on her arms, and a queer feeling had her stomach knotted up. She was indeed drawn to Wexford, far more than she'd ever intended, but now that her tendre had started, she had no desire to break it off. She wanted to see where it led.

Wexford might not think he was ready for a wife, or even a relationship, but Clare was certain if she kept his interest, he might eventually change his mind. For now, he interrupted her train of thought, not wanting her to stray too far from whatever it was they were talking about. He was doing his best to keep her mind off Francois, and she respected him for putting forth the effort.

"I suppose I should be getting you back," he said.

She nodded. "Yes. I must say, I've thoroughly enjoyed riding this fine mare."

"I'll remember that next time. She's one I purchased from Clevedon."

"That doesn't surprise me. He has exquisite taste in horses."

He shifted his weight in his saddle as they walked back toward the park entrance. "I understand I didn't bring you the news you wanted today, but I knew you would want to hear it from me."

"I am grateful, my lord. I was foolish. I realize that now, and I must move on."

"We all look back on mistakes we've made and wonder what we were thinking at the time. It makes us a better person."

She inclined her head. "Yes, yes, it does."

A short ride later, Clare dismounted the mare with Wexford's assistance. "Will I see you at the theater this evening?" Clevedon had secured a box for the season from a childhood friend who was visiting India. There was a Shakespeare work being presented, and the duke wished to see it. Clare also knew her cousin was using the evening to get her seen by the ton, and perhaps by a suitable match.

"My sister Alexandria insisted I should get out more, so yes, I will be in attendance."

She smiled demurely. "Then I hope to see you there, Wexford. My cousin has a box. Perhaps you'll come say hello to Clevedon."

"I shall make a point of doing so," he replied.

5

W exford had wanted to be anywhere but at the theater with his sister and her husband, Viscount Sansbury. His sister was not one to be easily put off. She was resolved he should get out more socially, but Wexford saw right through Alexandria. Her mothering instincts had kicked in, and she was determined to see him married again.

She and her husband had been invited to the Viscount and Viscountess of Hertford's box. Dread enveloped Wexford as he remembered the viscountess had been quite adamant about introducing him to her sister, Lady Henrietta Smith.

He followed his sister and the viscount into the box. Lady Hertford smiled the moment she saw him, dragging behind her a mousy young woman who had to be her sister.

Introductions were made, and the viscountess, eager to make a match for her sister was sure to seat them together in the front where everyone would of course see them. Wexford accepted a glass of champagne being served. Lady

Henrietta took a glass of punch and fidgeted, looking terrified at the thought of a man seated so closely.

Wexford's attention strayed to a box across the theater. Lady Clare sat there, her eyes meeting his. She winked naughtily in his direction, obviously amused that he'd fallen victim to the viscountess and her quest.

The viscountess had joined them, making small talk with Lady Henrietta, which was when Wexford realized what lengths his hostess would go to to see her sister married to someone like him. A step up in the peerage.

"Lord Wexford will be at the Duke of Liverpool's ball and has promised to sign your dance card for, I believe, two dances," she said boldly, her eyes locked with Wexford's.

Rather than answer, Wexford rose from his seat. He had to get out of there. He couldn't be a part of such schemes. He found his own sister before exiting the box. "Give my apologies, but I will not be part of this woman's plotting," he whispered.

"You cannot leave, brother. That would be rude."

"So be it," he replied.

Once out of the box, he headed down the stairs to take some air. He disliked social events such as this, but even more so because women were now plotting to see him remarried.

Clevedon must have observed what was transpiring from his box and had come in search of him. "I see the women are circling," he remarked with a slight smile.

"Yes, and I'm afraid I was rude to the chit."

"I'm sure you'll make it up to her at the Liverpool ball," he replied. "Come, you can sit with us."

Wexford nodded. "Thank you. I feel as though I was ambushed by my own sister."

"She just wants what's best for you."

"And in this case, that includes finding me a new wife."

Clevedon's eyebrows rose ever so slightly. "Ah, well, I must warn you Lady Clare joined us this evening."

"That's no problem. At least I can have an intelligent conversation with her."

"True, and Lady Clare's tongue is not as sharp as it was."

"Hard to believe."

Clevedon snorted. "Oh, I can assure you, she still has her moments."

Wexford stopped in his tracks. "My sources have confirmed her French paramour left over a week ago, heading to New York City."

Clevedon stopped at the door. "Good riddance. Her father will breathe easier. And you informed Lady Clare of your findings?"

"Yes, and she took the news far better than I expected. Perhaps she too is ready to let the matter go and move on."

The tension in the duke's shoulders eased. "That is good to hear. Please do apprise me if any further information comes from your investigations."

Wexford decided he shouldn't go into further detail regarding the young man. There would be more questions, and he felt like he'd be betraying Clare's trust. A trust he desperately felt he must keep. "I hope that will be an end to the matter."

The duke opened the door to the box. "Shall we join the ladies?"

All eyes were on them as the two men entered. Clare stared at him, her lips parted and shaped into a O. He shifted his eyes back toward Clevedon, who handed him a glass of whiskey. He gladly accepted and drank the contents in one swallow. He knew as soon as he sat down that his sister and the viscount and viscountess, along with the viscountess's cousin, would know that he'd abandoned them for his own friends. He hadn't meant to embarrass his sister; it was just that he could not abide the thought that, once again, someone thought he needed to remarry.

Mourning had been far easier than this. Being wrapped in gloom allowed him to keep out the world. The only shining light had been meeting Clare. She had lifted him out of the fog that had surrounded him. It was time, time for him to reassert himself. No one understood what he'd been through all those months, and he wasn't about to have those close to him assume what or who he needed in his life.

He accepted another glass of whiskey before finding his way to the empty chair beside Clare. Had it been empty all this time? He couldn't recall. He simply felt he had to be near her, as though she could shield him from the world.

"Was it getting a bit crowded over there?" she asked quietly as she kept her gaze fixed to the stage below.

"You saw that?" he muttered.

"I and everyone else, I'm afraid."

He pretended to be enthralled with what was going on below him, but his focus quietly shifted across to the box he'd just run from. He could only hope that with the lights turned down, his sister hadn't yet seen where he was. For now, he only wanted to get lost in another world. One that included Clare.

"I felt as though I were being smothered. I had to get some air, so I left."

"I'm not judging you. Merely making an observation," she replied with a smile that gave him hope. Hope that there was a chance for him to find love again.

He nodded. "Thank you." He studied her in the soft

light. Her ginger hair was swept up off her neck, and he found himself wondering what it would be like to kiss her there. He desperately would like to do so. But now was not the time, and any such inappropriate thoughts needed to be tucked away. Tonight, he was simply grateful he'd found Clevedon and that his friend had rescued him from an uncomfortable evening. He knew someone would be offended by his actions, but he didn't care. For once, he needed to think about himself and what he wanted. Not what others, including his sister, thought he wanted or needed in his life now.

He looked down at the actors on the stage and listened as Lady Clare quietly explained what was going on and where the play was set. The sound of her voice soothed him, making him realize just how long it had been since he'd relaxed and enjoyed himself.

Shortly thereafter, it was time for a short intermission. He stood to allow the two ladies to pass and head out into the hall. He felt as though someone was staring at him. As he dared to glance up, his eyes were met with the glaring orbs of his disapproving sister and the viscountess. He pretended he hadn't seen her staring and turned his back, walking farther in the box, where he found Clevedon mulling over a spread of food set out for their enjoyment.

"Not feeling so trapped?" the duke casually remarked.

"Amazingly, no."

"You're going to have to assert yourself, I'm afraid. I almost let grief consume me once. You can't let it do the same to you."

"I can assure you, it has nothing to do with grief, Clevedon. I'm afraid I've let my sister interfere where I don't need her. I must put a stop to it before she gets out of control."

"Lady Alexandria means well."

"She does, but still she insists on trying to pair me off with a new wife. When the time comes, I don't plan on allowing anyone else to choose for me."

Clevedon offered a plate to Wexford, who took it and mulled over his choices. He picked up some cheese and fruit. He hadn't realized he was hungry until now. He accepted a glass of champagne and stood to one side of the box as the ladies reentered and, chattering among themselves, began filling their plates.

"Are my eyes deceiving me, or is there something developing between you and my cousin?" Clevedon asked quietly. His lips formed a sly smile as he took a polite sip of champagne.

"I think Lady Clare and I have come to an understanding."

"Really? What sort of understanding would that be?" Clevedon asked.

Wexford quirked a brow. "We've become civil toward each other."

"Yes, I haven't heard her use her sharp tongue around you of late. I must say I find it refreshing."

"I can't take all the credit. In getting to know Lady Clare, I've come to the conclusion that being so headstrong and opinionated, her solution was to lash out with an acid tongue. I treat her as my equal, which I'm afraid is something no man, including her Frenchman, has ever done."

"Ah, that makes complete sense now that you explain it in that light."

"I take it her father has always treated her as merely his daughter, someone who should have no opinions about anything outside the normal life of a young lady."

Clevedon nodded. "Yes, I'm afraid the duke is a bit harsh with Lady Clare, but she's learned to placate him."

"How's does she do that?"

"She doesn't ask many questions, and keeps her thoughts to herself."

"What does he disapprove of? She's quite delightful once you get to know the real Lady Clare."

"She reads books a lady should have no interest in, she rides astride and has interest in bloodlines, things again a lady shouldn't know."

He nodded, thinking that those were among the very qualities he enjoyed most about her.

"Come, let us join the ladies before the next half of the play begins," Clevedon whispered.

Wexford nodded and made his way to the empty seat next to Lady Clare. Though her eyes never left the stage, she acknowledged his presence with a smile. When he sat next to her, the fragrance of oranges and vanilla caught his senses. So like her not to wear something floral and more traditional. He was quickly learning Lady Clare was in every way her own woman.

The next act began, and he quickly became enthralled by the drama.

"Have you ever been to Shakespeare's home, Stratford-upon-Avon?" he whispered.

She leaned closer to him. "I've not had the pleasure."

"With your love of history, you need to make at least one trip there."

"I'll take that under advisement. Would you accompany us if I could ask my cousin and his wife to take me? I know the duchess hasn't been either."

He nodded. "I would love to join you."

Wexford decided he would also make mention to Clevedon that Lady Clare and Her Grace might also enjoy an outing to Greenwich. Both outings would allow him and

Lady Clare the opportunity to get to know each other better. Far from the ballrooms and tearooms, they'd be free to enjoy stimulating conversation they might otherwise not have under the prying eyes of the ton.

CLARE AWOKE TO THE SOUND OF HER LADY'S MAID THROWING open the heavy drapes in her bedchamber. The sun shone through the windows. She loved the morning sun, especially when the light came into her chambers. It always made her feel renewed.

She slowly sat up, then swung her legs over the side of the bed. "The blue-and-white morning dress, and make sure the emerald dress is pressed. The duchess and I are having tea at Lady Thornwell's this afternoon."

"Yes, my lady. That color is striking on you."

Clare said nothing but took care of her personal needs before dressing for breakfast. The evening at the theater had proven to be quite enjoyable. She hadn't expected Wexford to be there, but he was. The poor man was being surrounded by women who thought he needed to remarry, which led him to escaping his own box last night and finding refuge in Clevedon's.

Certainly, she would like to marry one day, and Wexford was a distinct possibility. She just wasn't going to be like the other piranhas circling Wexford's leaking dingy, if one could describe it metaphorically. He'd shown an interest in her, and the best way to encourage him was to let him know just enough and not be obvious.

The Duke of Liverpool's ball was tomorrow night, and she knew everyone who was anyone would be there, including Wexford. It was one of the premier balls of the season and one to which everyone hoped to be invited. The crème de la crème of society would be in attendance.

She and Wexford already had an understanding regarding her dance card in case he couldn't reach her in time to sign it himself. The supper dance would be his, along with one other. Two was just enough for everyone to know he held an interest in her, but not enough to be scandalous. Clare shook her head at how silly society could be with their rules and expectations. Even in Edinburgh it was the same, though perhaps not quite as bad. She would get through it, as would Wexford.

The earl hadn't formally asked Clevedon or her if he could court her, but Clare felt it was just a matter of time. She'd asked herself several times if that was what she wanted. Each time the positive list far weighed the cons in Wexford's favor.

He'd been persistent and had shown himself to be a caring, attentive man who realized she wasn't one of those hothouse flowers that had to be handled with care. He embraced the idea that she was her own woman with her own thoughts.

She entered the breakfast room and found both Clevedon and his bride enjoying their breakfast together. She sat and waited for a footman to bring her a plate. Normally, she only had toast and eggs this early in the day.

"Good morning," the duchess said with a smile. "Are you ready for Lady Thornwell's tea?"

Clare smiled. "As much as anyone can be. I detest sitting around and listening to gossip."

"There will be plenty of that this afternoon, I'm sure."

A footman poured her tea while another placed a plate in front of her. "I enjoyed last evening. The play was quite well done."

Clevedon, who'd be hiding behind a newspaper, put it down to one side. "Wexford suggested we might all go to Stratford-upon-Avon for an outing since neither of you have been."

"I would love that," the duchess replied.

"Yes, I would love that as well," Clare said. She was thankful Wexford had put the gears into motion.

"He also thought you ladies might enjoy an outing to Greenwich one afternoon."

"I've heard it would be perfect for a picnic," the duchess gushed.

"I'll make some inquiries regarding both and see if we can schedule them soon," Clevedon mused with a sly glance at Clare.

Drat, there would be no fooling her cousin. He was probably acutely aware of what was going on right under his nose. He had, after all, known about Francois, because her father would have told him. Wexford was his friend, one he thought a great deal of.

He went back to reading his newspaper. She and the duchess grinned at each other as Clare slathered marmalade on a piece of toast and the duchess took a sip of tea.

"Do you think we'd have time to stop at that bookstore we passed the other day?" Clare asked as a deterrent from a conversation that might include Lord Wexford.

"Do you have something specific you're looking for?" Her Grace asked.

"No, the shop merely interested me."

"I see," the duchess replied. "Then may I suggest we go another time, when we can devote more time to looking through it?"

Clare nodded. "Of course."

After a moment, the duke folded his newspaper and set it on the table. "If you ladies will excuse me, I have an appointment with my tailor this morning."

He retreated from the room. Clare knew she had an ally in her cousin and his wife.

6

It was time for the Duke and Duchess of Liverpool's ball. As always, it was a grand affair. To some, an invitation meant that they had made their way to the top of London's society. It was the season's pinnacle event, with hundreds of distinguished guests.

At precisely half past eight, the affair began. Lady Clare entered the ballroom with her cousin and his wife, the Duke and Duchess of Clevedon. She tried to contain herself as she watched the pair walk arm and arm. The couple were so besotted with each other, Clare doubted another pair existed who were so in love.

Everyone was dressed in their finest. Ladies in shimmering new gowns were so beautiful, no man could keep their eyes off any one of them. The men were handsomely turned out as well. Some appeared to be quite comfortable in their surroundings, as though born for it. Others squirmed, clearly wishing they were anywhere else than at a ball.

Glancing around the ballroom, she caught sight of Lord Wexford to one side, alone. He seemed to be looking for someone. As their eyes met, he smiled and began to walk in her direction. Her heart skipped a beat as he neared. She quickly remembered the two dances she had promised him.

Just as Wexford was about to reach her, Octavos Burns, Marquess of Chatsford, stepped in front of her. It was a well-known fact the marquess was searching for a bride, one with a dowry large enough to pay off his numerous debts and shore up his estates. She'd heard her cousin make mention that bad business investments and gambling had gotten him in this predicament. She felt safe knowing that Clevedon would reject any request from Burns to court her. He was a strange-looking man, tall, with thinning brown hair, undistinguished brown eyes, and foul breath.

"Lady MacDougal, you're looking lovely this evening as always," he said with a curt bow.

"Thank you, Lord Chatsford."

"I was wondering if you would do me the honor of the dinner set?"

Wexford pushed the marquess aside, a smirk on his face as he watched the other man. He delighted in the marquess's reaction. "I'm sorry, my lord, but Lady MacDougal has promised me the dinner set as well as the first dance."

"Then how about the first set after dinner?" the marquess insisted.

Clare handed him the dance card and pencil. The marquess looked up at Wexford as he saw the two spots where Clare had penciled him in. "The second dance is a quadrille, my lord."

He begrudgingly signed his name for the second spot. "I look forward to our dance, Lady Clare," he said before bowing and walking off.

Wexford tried not to gloat over his small victory. "I suppose I should see what Lady Aston is waving at me for."

The duchess, who'd just joined Clare, smiled. "She probably wishes you to sign her two daughters' dance cards."

"*Two* daughters?" he groaned.

"Hyacinth and Marigold, I believe," the duchess replied. "Lovely girls, I understand, but in their fourth or fifth season, if I recall."

Wexford bowed at both women. "Wonderful. I'll try to remember that small fact."

Clare held out her hand. "I look forward to our first dance, my lord."

"As do I," he replied before walking off.

"Come," Savannah said. "We need to mingle, though I'm certain we'll shortly be surrounded."

"Why's that?"

"Because I'm an oddity. People are always curious about Americans. They imagine us to be wild heathens or something."

Clare giggled and smoothed the skirts to her sapphire silk ball gown. It was one of her newest, and the first time she'd worn it. The bodice was cut a little lower and tighter than she was used to, but the modiste insisted the style was all the rage in Paris and the rest of the Continent. It certainly seemed to be attracting the attention of the men. It was hard not to see them ogle her breasts as she and the duchess walked past.

Her dance card filled, Clare knew she could not spend the evening trying to hide. All her dance partners seemed to have one thing in common: they wished to gain her interest, and her sizeable dowry.

Before she knew it, her first dance with the marquess was being queued. A quadrille would at least keep the man at bay to some extent. She took his arm and let him lead her to the dance floor.

"You know, my dear, I don't believe there's actually a true dinner set as there is no formal dinner."

"And your point, my lord?" she asked coolly.

He smirked. "I realize you're a Scot and don't understand how the ton works here in London, but we're sticklers when it comes to social conventions."

"I can assure you, my lord, I know exactly how the ton works. London or Edinburgh, it makes no difference."

His brows knitted in disapproval. "I should like to call on you tomorrow. Perhaps I could take you for a drive."

"I'm sorry, my lord, but my day is filled," she lied. Under no circumstances would she be seen in public with this bore.

He smirked again. "We'll see what your cousin the duke has to say about all this."

"I can assure you he'll respect my wishes," she spat.

"Let me be clear, Lady Clare. I'm looking for a wife and intend to ask your cousin for permission to court you. If he should deny me, I'll simply bide my time until your father returns."

"Trust me, my lord, it'll be a cold day in hell that I allow you to court me."

"That's what I love. Your wildness. Which I will tame. It's what women like you need. The strong hand of a husband."

Clare said nothing for a few breaths. Anything she might say, he would simply counter. He wanted a possession, not a wife, and he wanted a wealthy one. Love meant nothing to this prig. "I can see trying to reason with you is futile."

"Women have their place, and it's long past due for you to learn yours. I'll change all that after we're married."

Clare laughed in his face. She hadn't meant to, but the

man was not worthy of a meaningful conversation. The dance was ending, and with it, she unleashed one last barb. "How presumptuous of you, my lord. It'll be an even colder day in hell that I marry you."

She returned to the area where she'd last seen her cousin speaking with Wexford and a small group of men. Clevedon knew her well enough to know she was displeased. He would never allow the marquess to come calling.

THE MUSICIANS WERE ABOUT TO BEGIN THE NEXT DANCE, which was a waltz. Wexford took her hand and led her out onto the dance floor. He placed his hand at her waist, and she moved with him as though they were one. She responded exactly as he'd anticipated. Couples whirled by as they spun and twirled. She was perfect in every way imaginable.

"You looked as though you were going to bite someone's head off, so I thought I should rescue you."

"Five more minutes with that prig and I would have devoured him," she replied.

Wexford arched a brow. "He insulted you?"

"Intentionally, I'm sure. He made it quite clear what a woman's place is."

"Yes, he appears that type," he replied.

"He intends to ask my cousin's permission to court me."

"Somehow, I can't see Clevedon allowing that. It's a well-known fact the marquess is looking for a woman with a substantial dowry as he's deep in debt."

"If my cousin says no, Chatsford will simply wait for my father to return."

"If you'd like, I could speak with the duke and let him know what may transpire this evening."

She nodded. "I would appreciate it. I'm sure Clevedon knows something is amiss, but hearing it from you might also help."

"Consider it done, and don't worry, Clevedon isn't going to allow this."

"Thank you," she whispered.

The waltz continued, and Wexford felt her relax in his arms the more time that passed. He glanced across the dance floor where he'd last seen the duke, and was surprised to see the marquess at Clevedon's side, speaking with him. The man was trying to make some point with the duke, for he saw Clevedon glance in their direction. A sinking feeling hit his gut. Chatsford had wasted no time in his pursuit of Lady Clare.

He had to protect her at all costs. She would never be happy with Chatsford, and forcing her into a marriage she did not want would destroy her spirit. She would be just another possession to the marquess, one with a sizeable dowry.

Too soon, the dance ended. She looked up at him as he returned her to her cousin-in-law, who stood waiting as she spoke with a pair of other women.

"I notice Chatsford wasted no time seeking out my cousin."

He nodded. "Yes, so it would seem. I'll find Clevedon and see if I can discover what the marquess said. That is if you don't mind."

"Please do, then make an excuse to escort me for refreshments."

He left her with the duchess before he sought out Clevedon. At least if he spoke with the duke on his cousin's behalf, Clevedon wouldn't allow Chatsford to court her. He found the duke speaking with a couple of men he did not know. He caught Clevedon's eye, beckoning him to seek him out.

"Chatsford has expressed a strong interest in my cousin," he said solemnly.

"I hope you discouraged him. Lady Clare wishes to have nothing to do with him."

"He didn't like what I had to say to him and informed me he would go straight to Clare's father."

"Just as Lady Clare predicted."

The duke cocked his head. "He wanted to call on her tomorrow afternoon, but I told him Her Grace and I had made other plans to take her to meet another cousin. It seemed to appease him, but I'm afraid I won't be able to hold him off past tomorrow."

"She has the right to refuse him if he calls on her," he said.

"As I expect her to, but he won't be deterred for long. He's known the duke for a good many years, and he'll simply write him and wait on a reply, or he'll wait for the duke to return," Clevedon said solemnly. "That's why I'm simply a pawn in his game."

He glanced across the room. Chatsford was talking with two other men, who fawned over him as though he were the most important man in the room. Disgusting. "Lady Clare will never agree to any of this."

"If you're the least bit interested in Clare, you must act, and act quickly."

It was then that Wexford realized what his friend was saying. The marquess meant to marry Lady Clare, and if Wexford had the slightest inclination toward taking her for his wife, he must act now. But was taking a wife so soon after a period of mourning had ended what he wanted?

"You can put him off, can't you?" he asked the duke.

Clevedon nodded. "Yes, but only for a short period of time. He's a business associate of Lady Clare's father. He's also ruthless when he wants something."

Chatsford might be ruthless, but Wexford was as well.

7

Three days after the ball, the duchess and Lady Clare sat in the drawing room. It had rained nonstop since the Liverpool ball, adding to Clare's already anxious mood. Wexford had called on her the first two days, bringing her flowers and a book of sonnets by Shakespeare. He was one in a long line of possible suitors. She had no interest in anyone but Wexford, and graciously sent the others on their way.

The Marquess of Chatsford was the only one who remained persistent. He ignored Clare's wishes and continued to call on her. Every day, he would ask to see her cousin, and each day, Clevedon was away on business.

Today, Clare had taken the drastic measure to refuse all visitors. She was sure she would die from boredom brought on by the marquess's monotonous drone on how incredibly wealthy he was. She knew it to all be a lie. A ruse to trick her. He thought her another woman without sense when it came to anything outside of a household, and from their earlier discussion at the ball, she wasn't going to anger him.

Though perhaps she should. Perhaps then he'd give up and move on to another woman.

She was pouring tea for herself and the duchess when Clevedon entered. He sat next to his wife, facing Clare.

"I have some news," her cousin began. "I received word from your father."

"Is everything well?" Clare asked.

"Yes. His correspondence is about the Marquess of Chatsford."

"Don't tell me, the marquess has been in touch with him, though I don't see how he could have a reply so soon."

"The marquess has asked your father for his blessing to marry you."

Clare stared at her cousin in disbelief. "So he bypassed you, knowing my father had trusted your judgment."

Clevedon nodded. "I'm afraid so."

"What did the duke say?" the duchess asked.

"He acknowledged the marquess's request, but told him I had been left in charge of the matter in his absence."

"I'm sure that didn't deter Chatsford," Clare whispered.

"No, it didn't. Your father went on to say that the marquess insisted on an answer from him."

"He's not going to win favor with my father."

"No, he isn't, but your father has asked me to allow the marquess to call on you."

Clare looked horrified. She set down her cup of tea. "What? I won't receive him. It'll only be encouraging him"

"I agree. There is, however, another problem."

"I can't imagine what," Clare choked out.

"I received word from Wexford this morning. It seems his grandmother is gravely ill, and he's leaving for Yorkshire this afternoon."

Clevedon pulled a note out of his pocket and handed the paper to her. "He sent this, and had flowers delivered a few moments ago."

Clare broke the seal and scanned the contents. She smiled and folded the paper. "He merely explains the matter of his grandmother, and that he'll return as soon as possible."

"If you wish to write him, I'll make sure it's delivered to him before he leaves."

"Yes," she replied. "This is only going to encourage the marquess. Once he learns Wexford is out of town, he's going to be relentless."

"Yes, I'm sure he will be." He smiled.

"What are you grinning about, cousin?"

Clevedon put his usual stone face back on. "I have written to your father in detail about the marquess and his refusal to accept your wishes. I also told him I thought Wexford to be the better match for you."

"You did?"

He nodded. "Yes. If you have to marry, I'd much rather see you married to an honorable man like Wexford than a man who sees women as their property and broodmares. I told your father as much."

"Thank you," she said quietly.

"So now what?" the duchess asked. "With Wexford headed out of town, how do we keep Chatsford at bay?"

"She's right," Clare said. "He won't take no for an answer with his competition out of the way."

"Your father informed me that if you were to choose Chatsford, he would have papers drawn up limiting how much of your dowry he can receive at once."

"Can he do that?"

"Considering Chatsford's financials are well known, yes."

Clare nodded. She knew her father and his reputation for being a meticulous businessman. He would not just sign over her dowry.

Simmons, Clevedon's butler, entered the drawing room and closed the door behind him.

"What is it, Simmons?"

"The Marquess of Chatsford is here to see you, Your Grace."

"Put him in my study and tell him I'll be with him momentarily."

Simmons bowed and quit the room.

"I'll leave you ladies with something to think about Clevedon said. "How would you like to go to Brighton? I can rent us a house overlooking the water. It's a delightful little town, from what I've been told."

"We'll discuss it," the duchess replied, as she tried not to smile too broadly.

Clevedon rose to leave the room. "I'd best not keep the marquess waiting. Heavens know I don't want him thinking I'm being rude."

"I'll have a reply for Wexford momentarily," Clare replied.

As the door closed, Clare went to sit at a small white writing desk. She opened Wexford's note and reread it. "You care a great deal for him, don't you?" she heard the duchess say quietly.

"I do. In spite of our rough start, I've found him to be someone with whom I can easily talk." She took out a piece of paper and began to write.

"Would you ever consider marriage to Wexford?"

"I'm not sure the earl even knows what he wants right now."

The duchess nodded. "Men seldom do. It's up to us to show them." She smiled as she poured another cup of tea.

Clare reread what she'd just penned. "What do you think of Clevedon's idea of going to Brighton? It's farther than a day trip, but it would be well worth the journey."

"I think it would be wonderful since any trips we planned with Wexford have now been put on hold."

Clare folded her note and readied it. "I agree."

"You're still worried about the marquess?"

"Yes. He's not one to take no for an answer."

"Don't despair, Clevedon will set him straight."

"I still don't trust him. Mark my words, when he learns we've gone to Brighton, he'll show up. He's like a dog with a bone. He won't give it up."

"Let's see what the duke learns. You can inform him of your concerns then."

"Agreed," Clare replied. "Do you know anything about Wexford's grandmother?"

"No, I'm afraid not. You'll have to ask Clevedon."

Clare stood, walked over to the wall, and rang. In a moment, a footman opened the door with Simmons following.

She handed him her missive. "Please see this goes out. I would like the earl to receive it before he leaves for Yorkshire."

The footman bowed under the watchful eye of Simmons. "Yes, my lady."

———

Wexford climbed into his carriage. He'd hoped the weather would clear. The idea of being stuck inside and unable to ride his horse was quite unnerving He'd brought his stallion on the off chance the weather improved.

As he began to settle himself in for the long journey, his butler opened the carriage door and passed him a note. He broke the seal and began reading. It was from Lady Clare.

She wished him a safe journey and that she looked forward to seeing him upon his return. He folded her note and placed it in the inside pocket of his jacket. He would respond when he arrived in Yorkshire.

His grandmother resided in one of the earldom's lesser estates and had since his grandfather died some years ago. She was his maternal grandmother and had always been there for him and his siblings, especially after their parents died. Her love was unconditional, whereas his paternal grandmother thought children should be seen and not heard, and that any special attention given them made them weaker.

The contrasts in the two women were astonishing. They were like night and day. Unfortunately, his father's mother had died five years ago after a lengthy illness. He prayed his grand-mère would have a speedy recover. Normally an active woman who worked in her own garden, much to the astonishment of her gardeners, she'd slowed down considerably after this past winter. Whether it was due to her advancing age or something else, Wexford was unsure.

He simply could not imagine his life without her and wanted nothing more than to have her meet Lady Clare, sure that the two would have a great deal more in common than just him. But her lady's maid had gone behind her back and written him, voicing her concern after the older woman had spent the warm weather indoors more than out with her prized rosebushes.

He knocked on the roof of the carriage, letting his driver know he was ready to begin the long journey north. The rain showed no signs of relenting, so he pulled the drapes closed to help keep out the dampness and allow him to sleep, if that were even possible. Sleeping in a carriage was a feat he'd never managed.

The traffic out of town was slow and unforgiving. The carriage would barely move forward, then all of a sudden, they were on their way briskly forward once again. If this journey was for anyone other than his grand-mère, he would have waited another day.

He prayed for sleep to pass the time as he was not in the mood to read either of the two books he brought along. He grew weary of the jerking as the carriage stopped and started. Soon, though, it began to pick up pace, and Wexford relaxed, knowing they were on their way north.

His thoughts began to drift to Clare. He found himself wondering what she was doing at this very moment. He hadn't been away long enough to miss her, but his heart felt an emptiness knowing he'd had to leave her, even for a day. He'd grown that fond of her. She was all the things Matilda had never been. Clare was full of life, excited to try new things, and could hold a conversation better than some of his contemporaries. She was well-read, and had read books most women would never dare pick up.

She was also the most exquisite creature he'd ever known. Not delicate like most cultured young women. She wasn't afraid to ride a horse in a hearty gallop across a meadow in the morning, and at night show off her voluptuous curves in one of those magnificent ball gowns she wore.

A smile crossed his face as an image of Clare racing across the grass on the gray mare he'd chosen for her came to mind. For now, this was all he had of her: his thoughts and memories. Soon, he would join her along with the duke and duchess, and he would make a concerted effort to know everything there was to know about this ginger-haired beauty.

8

Clare and her sister-in-law, Her Grace the Duchess of Clevedon, arrived in Brighton without incident. The sun came out shortly before they arrived in the seaside community. The carriage came to a stop in front of a stately manor situated near the water's edge.

Clare marveled at how majestic the house looked with the sandy beach as a backdrop. Her cousin had rented it for a fortnight, which was more than enough time to relax and take in the sea air. She'd seen similar houses near the beach at Edinburgh, but nothing quite as grand or new as this one.

Each lady was assisted from the carriage by a waiting footman. As they entered the house, instructions were being shouted as to where luggage should go. They'd each brought their lady's maid and left them to sort things out as Clare and Savannah walked through the grand hall and were shown to the drawing room.

Savannah promptly ordered tea for them, to allow their maids a chance to unpack. As they waited, they stood in front of the French doors and marveled at the sight of the water lapping up on the sandy shoreline.

"This is perfect," Savannah murmured. "I can't wait to walk along the water's edge."

"You've never seen the ocean in America?"

"I have, many times. I was named after the city of Savannah, Georgia. It's just been a while since I've laid eyes on it. It's not the same in eastern Scotland."

"No, it's not, is it? At least we can enjoy our time here without the likes of the marquess intruding on our day," Clare said.

Both women giggled at how deceptive they had been to the man. He deserved it. The moment he'd learned Wexford left town to check on his ailing grandmother, the marquess had called on Clare. She had rebuffed him each of the three times he'd appeared on their doorstep. On one occasion, she'd been out of the house, and the other two, she wasn't feeling well. Women's issues.

If he did find out where she'd gone, they might have to leave. Clare had no intention of going anywhere with the man or allowing him to call on her as he surely would. He was presumptuous and cold. He thought he could bypass her cousin and get permission to court her from her father. So far, her father had agreed to let Clevedon be the judge of who might make a suitable husband.

"What are you so deep in thought about?" Savannah asked.

"Wondering if Wexford has made it to Yorkshire and how his grandmother fares."

"He probably hasn't arrived. He'll send word to you."

The door opened, and a footman carried in a large tray, setting it down at a table in front of two settees. Savannah dismissed the man and walked to the tray to pour tea.

"How about we go for a stroll on the beach after we change?" Clare asked. She knew it was at least a three-day journey to Yorkshire. Until she heard from Wexford, she needed to keep herself occupied.

Savannah passed her a cup of tea and then took a seat to enjoy hers. "Clevedon said he'd join us in a day or two. There were a couple of business matters he wanted completed before he left on holiday."

"That'll leave us some time to shop."

"I thought we might do that tomorrow, as well as dine outdoors."

Clare nodded and sipped her tea. "Don't feel you have to entertain me once Clevedon arrives."

"Trust me, getting my husband to do anything that isn't related to business is nothing short of a miracle."

Clare found that hard to believe. Her cousin doted on his American-raised duchess. No, he was quite madly in love with Savannah and doted on her young son, Vincent. She had always hoped for a love match like they had. She felt she might find that with Wexford. Even her father would agree to that match.

"Come," the duchess said after they finished their tea. "Let's change, and I'll meet you in the grand hall in an hour."

Clare nodded. "I look forward to our walk."

"Before I go upstairs to change, I'm going to go introduce myself to the cook. I'd like to see what she intends for each meal."

"Very well. I'll leave you to your never-ending duties as duchess."

Clare headed up the stairs in the grand hall and found a footman at the top to guide her to her chamber. She was pleased with what she found, a light airy room done in pale yellows with a hint of blues. She hurried over to the windows and found the room overlooked the water and she could see beyond, toward a horizon that she assumed led to France.

The skies continued to show off the bluest of blues with puffy white clouds drifting by here and there. The sun shimmered on the water below, beckoning all to the shore. Here and there, couples walked up and down the beach, and she wondered where they'd come from or where they were headed.

She recalled Clevedon mentioning a beach that was open for those who swam or dared to enter the cold water. She would love the chance to wade in the water beyond her ankles. She smiled, thinking of Chatsford and how stuffy he was. She was sure a wife of his would never be allowed to do any of that, let alone taking her shoes off and walking through the water as it lapped on to the shoreline.

Octavos Burns, Marquess of Chatsford, stood on the terrace to the house he was to live in for the month he'd be in Brighton. The three-story brick home actually belonged to an old friend of his, Thomas Moore, the Earl of Greystone. The earl had graciously offered his manor house upon hearing Chatsford was traveling to Brighton as he and his wife had decided to travel to Italy for the summer.

He accepted a glass of whiskey a footman had brought him as he stood and watched the people walking along the shoreline. He knew through his sources that Clevedon's wife and cousin were staying in a house close by. He also understood that Wexford wouldn't be joining them as he'd traveled north to visit his ailing grandmother. Actually, as far as Chatsford knew, Wexford's grandmother was in perfect health. He'd merely constructed a ruse to get the man out of town and away from Lady Clare. Chatsford intended to make good use of the house and his stay in Brighton.

By the time he left Brighton, Lady Clare would be betrothed to him, or better yet, he would expose her to an improper situation and she would be forced to either save her family's good name and marry him, or find herself ruined.

Ruined was exactly what he had in mind. He would compromise her at just the perfect time. There would be plenty of opportunities, including a party he'd gotten himself invited to at Viscount Smith's Brighton home. The viscount's estate was farther inland, on a bluff overlooking the water. People from London would be attending, as most of the cities people fled to the coast in the warmer months. Knowing the viscountess, she would have games to keep the guests busy before dinner. A perfect scenario in which to take advantage of a young lady such as Clare.

The Duke of Clevedon had thwarted his every move he made to court Lady Clare. Chatsford simply went around the duke and directly to the chit's father, who was also a duke. A very wealthy one. He needed funds, and the easiest and quickest way to attain them would be to acquire the girl's dowry, which was one of the largest, and it would be his.

He had an inside source in the Clevedon's household, so learning what Lady Clare had planned for a day would be absurdly easy. He would simply show up on the beach when she and the duchess took their walks, or bump into them in town when they went shopping. The pittance he was paying the young maid was more than worth it.

He swallowed the remainder of the whiskey in his glass, then went to a wrought iron table where a crystal decanter sat and poured himself another. Chatsford knew the ladies would be walking along the shoreline. It was time to make himself known.

Not wanting to startle the women, he had come up with an elaborate ruse for why he was in Brighton at the exact same time they were. He would merely say hello, engage in small talk, and be on his way. Nothing out of the ordinary.

He smiled at the thought of Wexford hurriedly on his way north. Not until he arrived in York might he put together the pieces and discover he'd been played.

By the time Wexford spent a day or so with his beloved grandmother and returned to London, Chatsford would be married to Lady Clare. Wexford would have been too late by the time he finally did arrive in Brighton.

Chatsford set the glass down on the table and headed to the stairs, which led down to the beach. He knew where Clevedon had rented a house and began to walk in that direction.

Watching where people flocked, he decided being closer to the water was probably his best bet. Lady Clare seemed the sort who would dare take her boots off and wade in the waves. He smirked. Women were so predictable, even Lady Clare.

She wasn't the sort of woman with whom he usually associated himself. He preferred his women to be dainty and not likely to talk with him about much more than the weather or a book or play they might be interested in. Her ginger hair and dark green eyes were also out of character with women he'd courted in the past. Most had had flaxen hair and blue or hazel-brown eyes.

But he could overlook all her faults, especially her notoriously acid tongue, if it meant he would have control of her dowry. Besides, once he had her with child, he would send her to his estate outside Kent. After she had given birth, he would call on her and begin the process again. He needed an heir, actually two. If she bore him only daughters, he would see she remained pregnant until she fulfilled her obligation as his wife.

He walked along the sand. It was packed down where the water had recently lapped up on it and the sun hadn't dried it out. The tide was on its way out, meaning more people would come to walk along the water's edge. It was one of Brighton's largest attractions.

Chatsford had the sun to his back when Lady Clare first came into view. She had her skirts lifted with one hand and her boots in the other as she giggled every time the water splashed her feet. The duchess walked beside her, watching.

He approached slowly, carefully. "Your Grace, Lady Clare, this is indeed a pleasure, and a lovely surprise."

Lady Clare stared at him in disbelief. This was to be expected. Her Grace was far more reserved in her observation and greeting him.

"Lord Chatsford, indeed this is a surprise."

"How did you know we would be here?" Lady Clare hissed.

He bowed. "I can assure you, Lady Clare, I'm surprised to see you as well." Deciding he needed to leave in order to let his ruse play out, he bowed once again. "Ladies, if you'll excuse me. I have business in town."

The entire encounter was perfect. She knew he was here, and the next move would be to run into her and the duchess as they shopped. Perhaps he could then invite them for tea at one of the local bakeries. It mattered not; his plan was in place, and he wouldn't fail this time around.

Savannah and Clare stood in disbelief as they watched the marquess's figure disappear into the crowd. The duchess finally broke the silence.

"Come, we must return to the house. I must write to Gabriel and tell him we arrived safely and that the Marquess of Chatsford is here." The duchess lifted her skirts, and turned toward the house.

"There is no way he just happened to show up here at the exact same time," Lady Clare bit out.

"No, there isn't. My concern is how did he know we would even be here? It's not as though we announced it among the ton."

Lady Clare struggled to keep up with her cousin's wife, who was far angrier than she. Nothing the marquess did was coincidental. The duchess was right. As far as she knew, no one except Wexford and Clevedon were aware they were in Brighton.

"Can you get word back to London today?" Clare inquired.

The duchess stopped and turned to Lady Clare. "Word

will reach him today, if I have to send a private rider. I have a bad feeling about this man being here. Clevedon has said he does nothing without reason that benefits him."

"Aye, and we know he is after my dowry."

"Well, he's not going to get it."

"I can imagine what Papa might have said."

The duchess smiled. "Indeed."

"Well, we know he's not going to do that. His being here is proof enough," Clare replied.

They approached the house and went inside. Clare hated the idea of being cooped up inside on such a beautiful day, but there were priorities to deal with first. She followed the duchess into the house and to the library, where she sat down at a small mahogany writing desk.

Finally she put the quill down. "How does this sound? 'Chatsford has shown up in Brighton. I fear he's up to no good. Please come as soon as you possibly can.'"

"It gives him enough information without going into details."

The duchess nodded. "Exactly. Clevedon knows anyway. What I still can't get out of my head is how did Chatsford even know we were here?"

"Perhaps he went to your home and found out we'd left."

"No, the staff is far more discreet than that. They would have only mentioned you and I were out of the house. That could imply all sorts of things. We were out for the afternoon, we were shopping. No, I don't worry about my staff."

Clare watched as the duchess folded the missive and seal it with wax. She picked up a bell at the side of the desk and rang. A moment later, the butler appeared. She gave implicit instructions that the missive was to be sent out to London using someone from her staff which had accompanied them.

"This must reach my husband today. Send our best and fastest rider as soon as possible."

"As you wish, Your Grace." The butler picked up the sealed paper, bowed, and left the room. Clare smiled. There were some advantages to being a duchess. Everyone was at her bidding.

The duchess stood and walked toward Clare. "I believe I'm going to lie down for a while. The ride from London and the sea air has tired me. I'll have tea served in the drawing room at four. We can decide what we want to do then."

"I think I'll do the same in a few minutes. I thought while I'm here, I'd make a list of just that."

"I thought you might. I'll also inform the butler we're not seeing anyone this afternoon. That way if Chatsford decides to be bold and come to call on you, he'll be sent away."

"Thank you."

The duchess smiled warmly. "No need to thank me. The man will not take no for an answer, and I intend to block every move he makes. Hopefully, Gabriel will arrive by tomorrow, or we'll at least hear from him."

"I'll be fine. Now go lie down. As soon as I'm finished here, I'll do the same."

Clare watched as the duchess glided across the rug and out the door. Her cousin had been fortunate to have met his American duchess. She was a breath of fresh air with her American accent and sayings. Clare enjoyed her tales about what life in America was like. She knew the duchess missed her life there, but was madly in love with Clevedon.

The pair never hid their devotion to the other. Each had endured a shattered past, losing a loved one of their own. But the two were inseparable. Clevedon doted on Vincent, Savannah's young son and earl to his father's family line.

Her mind shifted to Wexford. She hoped one day she would have such a love as her cousin, and perhaps it would be with Wexford. They hadn't gotten off on the right foot, but she had found herself impressed with him and the fact that he had interest only in her, and not her dowry. He wasn't a fortune hunter, unlike the Marquess of Chatsford.

———

THE EARL OF WEXFORD SLID OFF HIS STALLION AND HANDED the reins to a waiting stable boy. Fortunately, the weather had cleared and he'd been able to ride the black beast this past day. He hated being confined to a carriage, no matter how short the distance.

"How is my grandmother faring? What does the doctor say?" Wexford asked the butler as he handed him his gloves. He'd ridden, as always, without a hat, preferring to enjoy the feel of the wind blowing through his hair.

"I beg pardon, my lord, but there has been no need to call the doctor. Your grandmother is in perfect health, I can assure you."

Wexford stood in stunned silence. "I received a missive telling me to come quickly, that she was gravely ill. The signature was illegible, but I assumed it was from you or my estate manager."

The butler, White, shook his head. "I can assure you, my lord, nothing has been sent to you. If you'd like to see for yourself, the dowager countess is in her rose garden."

"Yes, but no need to alert her. I think I'd like to surprise her," he replied. "And, White?"

"My lord?"

"Not a word about this to anyone, especially the dowager. I need to find out what's going on."

He nodded. Wexford glanced at the man's salt-and-pepper hair. White had been with the family for years, going back all the way to when his grand-mère and grand-sire had first married. He strode across the grand hall, through the drawing room, and out the French doors overlooking the countess's prized rose garden. This one simple pleasure had always held her heart. No matter how bad things might get, if the roses were in bloom, and even if they weren't, you could find the dowager there.

She was cutting blooms when he came upon her. He'd tried to be as quiet as a church mouse, but the dowager's hearing was acute as ever. She smiled warmly and put the shears in the basket she carried.

"To what do I owe a visit from my favorite grandson?"

Wexford kissed her on the cheek. "Do I have to have a reason grand-mère?"

She shook her head of white hair. "Of course not. Never. You know how I enjoy your visits. Even if they are infrequent."

"You know that can't be helped," he replied. He looked down at her. She was a petite woman, and though in her eighth decade, she was still as spry and alert as she'd ever been.

"Come, let's get you settled in. Will you be here long?"

He hesitated. "I'm not sure. I need to write an associate in London before I make that decision. But as long as I'm here, you have my complete attention."

"After you write this associate."

"Yes, it's important and will only take a moment," he replied. "Why don't you ring for tea, and have Cook make some of those sandwiches you adore."

The older woman cackled. "I think you adore them far

more than I. But I'll do that and then wait for you on the terrace."

Wexford placed her hand on her arm. "Come, I'll escort you back to the house. Unless, of course, you are in need of more blooms."

"One can never get enough roses, but this will be fine for today."

He left his grandmother in the drawing room, where she was barking orders to her staff. Wexford smiled at how spry she still was, but was concerned over who had sent him north when his grandmother was not sick in the least.

He poured himself a whiskey and sat behind his desk in his study, found a sheet of paper and wrote Clevedon a missive. He explained what had occurred, that he'd been sent north for no reason and felt for sure Chatsford was somehow behind it.

The man wanted him out of the way so he could court Lady Clare, and what better way to do it than to send him rushing to his grandmother's side? It kept him on the road for days while Chatsford made his move.

The man certainly didn't listen. He had his own agenda, and with Lady Clare's father not getting involved while he was on the continent, he had to gain Clevedon's approval to court his cousin. The duke had no intention of allowing that to happen. He knew far too well the sort of man Chatsford really was.

When Wexford finished and the ink had dried, he folded the missive and poured wax, pressing it with his signet ring. He took a swallow of whiskey and rang for the butler.

"My lord?"

"I need to see this missive gets on the way to London immediately."

The older man picked up the sealed note and nodded. "I'll see to it immediately, Your Grace," he replied. "Would you care to change now? Your bags are in your suites."

"No, I promised my grandmother I would have tea with her as soon as I finished my business."

"Yes, the dowager does not like to be kept waiting," he replied.

Wexford nodded, and once the butler had closed the door behind him, he finished off the glass of whiskey. He had his suspicions of who'd sent him. Now he just needed proof. He also knew he needed to get to Brighton as soon as possible. Unfortunately, though, since he'd come all this way, his grandmother would expect him to stay with her for a few days. After which he could explain to her that something had come up at his Kent estate that needed his attention.

He stood and admired the taxidermy hanging on the walls, the old armor standing in one corner of the room and the threadbare rug on the floor. All reminders of just how long this estate had been in his family.

But memories and reminiscing were far from relevant to what was going on. He paced the floor. Damn Chatsford! The man might be thinking he'd won the battle over Clare, but it had only just begun. For him, there was no winning Clare over. Chatsford, on the other hand, would soon find that Lady Clare did nothing she didn't want to. That in itself gnawed at Wexford, because he knew Chatsford to be frantic for money, and desperate men did desperate things.

10

Clevedon arrived in Brighton a day later. Business of a disturbing nature had required his immediate attention. The duke had a financial interest in a shipping firm which ran between New York, Philadelphia, and Wilmington. The ports of entry were deliberate. Each was far enough apart they could serve the areas around them. A strategic move, with hopes of expanding over the next couple of years. America needed goods from England and the Continent, and Clevedon was eager to accommodate this need.

Unfortunately, he had received some unsettling news. One of their ships bound for New York had perished during a storm. Such an event was not unheard of, especially this time of year when bad weather sometimes plagued the Atlantic. The usual paperwork and filings would need to be done and customers notified in New York. Nothing unusual about this; he and his partner had people to take care of these matters.

However, this time, he had news about the crew and passengers, all of whom had been lost. One name in partic-

"What is it, Gabriel?"

Clevedon set the cup on a small table to the right of the doors, which were already open to allow the fresh air inside. "Chatsford, what the hell are you doing here?"

The marquess glanced up, a hand on Clare's shoulder as though he claimed her for his own. "I was walking past and saw Lady Clare sitting here sketching. I meant no harm."

"And get your hand off my person, sir. I've asked you twice. This time, I'll ask my cousin to assist me."

Chatsford slowly removed the hand in question from her shoulder. "What are you doing here, Clevedon? I thought you had business in London."

"My affairs are none of your concern, sir. The fact that you continue to bother my cousin does concern me. She told you she wasn't interested in you courting her, and that should be enough."

"I've contacted her father, and he has sided with me. I have his blessing to court your cousin."

Clare, who'd been listening all this time, slammed her sketchpad and pencil down on the table beside her. "Bloody hell, have you no shame? Enough of your lies, Lord Chatsford."

She stood and stormed back into the house, leaving both men watching as her figure disappeared.

"I'm afraid I must tell you to keep away from Lady Clare. Not only does she not wish for your courtship. *I* do not want you calling on her. Do I make myself clear?"

The man ran his fingers through his hair, which the wind had made unkempt. "Perfectly. This isn't over, Clevedon. Once her father returns, I can assure you the two of us will be betrothed and wed."

"My uncle loves his daughter far too much to condemn her to a life with you."

Without another word, Clevedon walked back inside. He turned at the doorway as soon as he was inside to make sure the marquess had indeed left, but the man was nowhere to be found. Clevedon knew this wasn't over. Chatsford would not rest until he had his way and Clare was his.

"He's gone. I reminded him once again you did not want his courtship. I doubt we'll see him darkening our doorstep anymore." Clevedon picked up his teacup and swallowed what remained. It was almost cold.

"He's a horrid man," Clare remarked.

"I don't want you going anywhere alone. If you're not with us, make sure your lady's maid accompanies you. I don't trust the man."

"I won't. You don't have to worry about that."

Clevedon accepted another cup of tea from his wife and sat down across from Clare. He knew he had to tell her about her Frenchman. He dreaded bringing it up, but it had to be done.

"I'm afraid I have a bit of news, Clare."

She rolled her eyes in disbelief. "Chatsford isn't enough? You have more?"

He nodded. "I'm not sure you know, but one of my businesses is a shipping firm. We specialize in shipping to America and bringing back goods and such from there. One of the ships was due in New York two weeks ago. It never arrived and is assumed lost at sea."

"That's awful."

"Francois Bernas was listed on the passenger-and-crew manifest," Clevedon said solemnly. "I'm so terribly sorry, Clare."

"So he did go to America. Without me," she said quietly. "Tell me, was he crew or a passenger?"

The duke took a sip of tea. "He was a crew member."

"How ironic. Our dream was to go to America, and he ends up perishing as a crew member on a ship belonging to a family member of mine."

Savannah reached out and took one of Clare's hands. "At least you know what happened to him. You won't ever have to wonder again."

Clare nodded, tears in her eyes. "That chapter of my life is now closed. It's time to move on."

―――――

WEXFORD ARRIVED LATE THE FOLLOWING MORNING. UPON deducing that news of his grandmother's illness was a ruse in order to keep him away from Lady Clare, Wexford had pushed his horse and his team to Brighton.

Clevedon met him in the drawing room.

"You look as though you've been riding for days. Please tell me you haven't," the duke said.

"I would have if there'd been a moon," he replied.

The duke walked to a sideboard and poured them both a whiskey. He handed a glass to Wexford as the two began to recount their steps. Chatsford indeed had to have been behind sending Wexford running to his grandmother's side.

Clevedon told him of Chatsford's escapades, showing up in Brighton and attempting to gain Lady Clare's attention. He mentioned the incident of the day before, where Chatsford simply appeared out of nowhere while Lady Clare had been sketching on the terrace.

"The man certainly has no intention of taking no for an answer," Wexford mused.

"No, he doesn't. He still thinks her father will allow this when her father made it abundantly clear that I'm her protector, and as such, can choose whom may court Clare."

Wexford took a swallow of whiskey. "You've told him to leave Lady Clare alone. Do you really think he's going to abide by your wishes?"

"No, which is what I want to speak with you about."

The earl took a seat in a nearby chair and waited for the duke to do the same.

"I know an attraction has formed between you and my cousin. If you're as interested in her as I believe you to be, I give my blessings and permission to court her."

"I don't know what to say. I had planned to ask you after I spoke with your cousin, of course. This is most unexpected and pleasing."

Clevedon swirled the whiskey in his glass and took a hefty swallow. "There is something else."

"What's that?"

He explained to Wexford about the ship he'd lost at sea and Lady Clare's young Frenchman being aboard. "My cousin was saddened, but she also has come to the conclusion that that chapter of her life is closed."

Wexford downed the last of his whiskey and set the glass on a nearby table. He ran his fingers through his windblown blond hair. "I hate to hear that, but am happy to see she realizes she must move on with her life."

"More whiskey? I feel as though a celebratory drink is called for." The duke poured them both another whiskey. "Tell me, do you have a place to stay?"

"No, I left in such a hurry, I failed to even think about such matters. I'm sure I can find suitable accommodations in town."

Clevedon took a long swallow of the amber liquid. "No need, we have plenty of room here. Let me find my wife. She can decide which bed chambers to put you in."

"Thank you. I'd be delighted to stay if it's not too much trouble."

The duke rose. "No trouble at all. In fact, I could use some male company, and I'm sure Lady Clare will be delighted to spend time with you."

After the duke left the room, Wexford found himself hoping that Clare was indeed glad to see him. They could take walks on the beach and he could take her to town. The thought of Chatsford still nearby tugged at him. The man surely wouldn't give up that easily, and that concerned him. He was sure the thought had also crossed Clevedon's mind as well.

Moments later, Clevedon, accompanied by his duchess, returned. The duchess, as always, was gracious.

"Dear Wexford, I was so distressed to hear your journey to York was nothing more than a way to lure you away from Clare."

"Fortunately, my grandmother was well and thriving."

"You must stay with us. I'll have a bedchamber readied for you. While you're waiting, I believe you'll find Lady Clare in the music room."

He cocked a brow. "Thank you. I think I'll check in on her."

The duchess smiled broadly. "I'll let you know when your rooms are ready. I'm sure you'd like to freshen up."

Clevedon, who'd been standing behind his wife with an arched brow added to the conversation. "We were planning on a quiet evening at home tonight."

"Tomorrow evening, the Viscount and Viscountess of Hertford are holding their summer ball. From what I understand, they open their ballroom doors so that guests can dance on the terrace. It's quite romantic, I'm told."

"I look forward to it." He bowed. "If you'll excuse me, I think I'll surprise Lady Clare."

Wexford followed the muffled sound of a piano being played down the hall. A piece by Bach, he mused, and Lady Clare's playing was better than that of most young women. Music was a very important part of Clare's formal education. Her parents had hired the finest tutors and teachers. It was obvious all the years of practicing and study had paid off. Only in a concert hall had he heard such perfection.

Quietly, he opened the door. Her back was turned to him as she continued to played.

When she stopped, Wexford politely clapped. "That was lovely. I had no idea you were so talented."

"Wexford!" she exclaimed. The next thing he knew, she was standing before him. "You're really here."

He felt his heart pound at the mere sight of her. It had been too long since he'd felt like this, since he'd ached to be near someone he truly cared deeply for. "Yes, I came as soon as I figured out Chatsford was behind everything. Clevedon explained what happened yesterday as well."

"That man is horrid."

He drew her hand to his mouth and kissed the back. "There is no reason for you to worry about him. He won't be bothering you again."

"Somehow, I'm not sure I believe Chatsford will give up so easily."

"Come, play more for me. Please."

"In a moment. There is so much to tell you."

He nodded. "Yes, I know."

"Clevedon told you about Francois?"

"He did," he replied.

"It made me sad, but I realize that relationship was doomed from the start."

He brushed his lips against hers, and she responded. The kiss deepened, but Wexford put an end to it. There would be plenty of time for that later. "Play more for me while I wait for my rooms to be readied."

"You're staying here?" She smiled.

"The duchess insisted, as did Clevedon."

Her tongue flicked over her pink lips, and her green eyes sparkled with mischief. "How scandalous, my lord."

He laughed and led her back to the piano. "Once I've had an opportunity to freshen up and change, we could take a walk on the beach. That is if you'd like that."

"I'd love to, though it'll have to wait until after our midday meal."

"And I'm famished," he replied.

She sat again at the keyboard. "Do you play, my lord?"

"Violin, but I must admit it's been quite a while since I picked one up, and I'm nowhere as good as you."

"I play violin as well. Harp too, though the piano is my favorite."

"It shows. You're magnificent."

She graced him with another smile. "Do you like Mozart?"

"Yes, though he can be rather dark in some of his pieces."

She began to play Mozart's Piano Sonata Number Eleven, known also as the Turkish March, which was a fairly popular piece. She needed no sheet music as her fingers flew across the keyboard. As he was enjoying the piece, someone knocked on the door and the butler appeared. Clare immediately stopped.

"Beg pardon for interrupting, my lady, but his lordship's rooms are ready. His valet is unpacking as we speak."

Wexford nodded and thanked the older man. He stood

as he waited for the door to close. "May we continue this later? I'll freshen up and meet you in the drawing room. I'm sure the meal will be served then."

"I look forward to it, my lord." She grinned and turned away, her face flushed, and began to play once again.

He was thankful for the diversion. Now that she'd agreed she wished him to court her, it was all he could do to keep his hands to himself, road dust or not. There soon would be time for that. He knew he needed to take it slowly, but his baser instincts told him otherwise. The idea that Chatsford had touched her made him less than happy.

No man would lay a hand on her again. He hoped their relationship would continue to deepen and marriage might be discussed. Not long ago, the idea of marrying again had been laughable. Getting to know Clare had softened his feelings. After Matilda's death, and his guilt over the accident, he never imagined he could love again. But now he could not imagine sharing a bed with anyone other than Clare.

His heart was set on her.

He'd already decided on the ride down from York that should Clevedon give his blessing he would see to it that the majority of her dowry were put in a trust for any daughters they might have. It was the least he could do. He didn't really need all that money, and having money set aside would assure their daughters would be well taken care of financially.

He followed the butler up the stairs and down a separate hallway, the guest wing, the man explained. The older gentleman swung open the door to a spacious room done in blue and golds.

"I hope this will meet with your approval, my lord."

Wexford saw his valet scurrying around near the

bathing chamber. The man knew him better than he knew himself sometimes. "It's quite nice. Thank you."

The butler nodded before quitting the room. "Luncheon will be served on the terrace, my lord. The family will gather in the drawing room in three-quarters of an hour."

"Thank you," he replied as he shed his jacket and began loosening his cravat. His mood was lighter now that he was in Brighton. The fact that he'd spent days on the road to return to Lady Clare's side was a distant memory. Certainly, he imagined he had been in love with Matilda, but his feelings had been nothing like this. He didn't recall his perception of love being anywhere near what he was feeling now. Was this what it meant to be in love? If it was, he didn't want it to end.

11

Viscount and Viscountess's Hertford's Brighton lavish summer parties were well known among peers. Everyone who was anyone vied for the coveted invitation. Far different from the stifling ballrooms of London, dancing at theirs was held on the large terrace which ran behind their summer home. Lanterns adorned the perimeter and down the stairs that led not only to the beach, but to small gardens. The shimmering light provided a romantic walk for couples.

Wexford and Clare had danced several times. Somehow, she had managed to make something he thought of as a task into something fun. She was light on her feet and felt wonderful in his arms. Wexford had decided to tell Clare of his discussion with her cousin after a waltz they shared. The sooner she knew and agreed, the easier he'd breathe.

Wexford placed her hand on his forearm and led her down the stairs toward the garden. A few other couples strolled leisurely, whispering and laughing together.

"It's a beautiful evening, isn't it," he remarked. When he sat next to her on the wood and iron bench, the fragrance of oranges and vanilla caught his senses. So like her not to wear something floral and more traditional. He was quickly learning Lady Clare was in every way her own woman.

"Yes. It's quite clever to move the dancing to the terrace. Makes it so much more enjoyable, don't you think?"

"It does," he replied. He hesitated for a moment before he stopped and pulled her off the path to an iron and wood bench. "Let's plan a picnic for tomorrow. I'd like to get to know you better, and for you to know me."

"I would like that, my lord. I've enjoyed our time together," Clare replied with a soft blush. "I see Hertford is trying to get your attention. If you'll excuse me, I'm going to freshen up. I promise to return in a short while."

He nodded and watched her as she walked away before he strolled across the gardens to Hertford and a couple other gentlemen who were talking with the viscount.

Everything about Clare was unique. He was able to converse with her on so many matters. Matters most women were told weren't subjects women, young ladies in particular should discuss with anyone, especially a man. She was smart, funny, beautiful and most of all her own woman. She was more than he'd ever dreamt possible.

SEVERAL MINUTES LATER, CLARE HADN'T RETURNED, CAUSING Wexford to worry. She'd been away far too long, and he decided he needed to try to find her. Besides, talk of politics and such bored him. In his orderly world, there was a time and a place for such discussions, and politics was not something to be talked about so openly.

Wexford was walking down the hall when he heard the faint cry of a woman in distress. Clare.

"No!"

He checked the rooms as he went until he found a door standing ajar. He entered to the sight of Clare struggling in Chatsford's arms.

"No!" she cried out.

The marquess had one hand on Clare's bare breast.

Wexford strode into the room and grasped him in rage. "How dare you!"

The look on Chatsford's face was one of smug arrogance. Wexford grabbed him hard by the arm and punched him in the face. The marquess stumbled back and fell.

The blackguard rubbed the back of his hand against his mouth. "She's ruined."

Wexford shed his coat and covered Clare. "Did he hurt you?"

"No, he accosted me in the hall and was trying to have his way with me."

"You lying little tart," Chatsford said from the floor. Blood streamed from his nose.

"Enough!" Wexford barked. He bent and hauled the marquess to his feet, then shook him hard. "She's told you over and over again that she does not wish your attention, and still you do not listen."

"She's ruined. Her father will see it that way and will give his blessing that we wed."

———

the face as hard as she could. "You're a disgusting little man."

Chatsford held a hand to his cheek. "This isn't over. I plan to write your father tonight."

By this time, the duchess had stumbled across the trio.

She rushed to Clare's side and began issuing orders to a shocked footman who stood at the door. "Please find my husband, the duke."

The marquess's eyes grew wide, but still he didn't give up. "Yes, fetch the duke. He'll see I'm right." He turned to Clare. "You'll see. We'll be married before you know it."

Clare tore away from the duchess and stormed over to Chatsford, who was being held upright by Wexford. She balled up her fist, and the next thing she knew, her fist met his nose. "You come anywhere near me, and I'll be sure to tell everyone what you've attempted here tonight."

"Bitch, you broke my nose." His nose was bleeding once more, and he'd have a good bruise. He held both hands his face as he attempted to stop the flow.

"That's the least of your problems," she hissed.

Clevedon arrived along with the footman. By now, it was well known something had happened. There was no keeping secrets, even in Brighton.

The duke strode over to Clare and his wife, who stood to one side. "Why don't you take Lady Clare somewhere more private and get her a brandy. Wexford and I will dispose of this insect."

Their hostess, Viscountess Hertford, lingered outside in the hallway, speechless at what had happened in her house. "Lady Clare, Your Grace, come with me."

The trio made their way up the stairs to a private family sitting room. The duchess helped Lady Clare sit on a red settee while the viscountess poured them each a brandy.

"I can assure you neither my husband nor I had the first inkling of Lord Chatsford's true colors. We wouldn't have invited him this evening if we had."

Clare graciously accepted the brandy snifter and took a small sip. "I'm sure you wouldn't have. My cousin the duke tells me Chatsford is destitute and has been seeking to marry a young lady with a large dowry."

"I've heard that as well."

The duchess sat ramrod straight. "My husband has told the marquess more than once that Lady Clare is under his protection while her parents are on the continent. He informed the man that any suitors were to go through him. Instead, the marquess has tried to bypass the duke. To no avail, I might add."

She nodded. "He's a wolf in sheep's clothing, isn't he?"

"He is that," Clare agreed. "I hope this time he gets the message."

"He won't want to deal with Clevedon if her persists. He's had about enough of the marquess's rudeness and lack of social graces."

"He may tell anyone in the ton who'll listen that he's ruined you. Some men are like that," the duchess added.

"Let him. I refuse to let my life be dictated by a man. I am just thankful Lord Wexford came across us when he did. I dread what might have happened if he hadn't."

The duchess smiled. "Wexford thinks quite highly of you. Not many men would come to a lady's rescue all the way from York. He did because he knew something was not right."

Clare knew she was right. Things could have turned out much differently, and she would always be in Wexford's debt. They'd gotten off on the wrong foot in the beginning, but he'd showed her nothing but caring and concern since then.

"I know. I can't believe the lengths Chatsford went to," Clare said as she brought the brandy snifter to her lips.

"What do you mean?" Viscountess Hertford inquired.

"For one, he sent Wexford rushing to York thinking his

grandmother was gravely ill. When he arrived, he realized it was all a ruse."

"That's horrible."

"Plus he's been corresponding with my father, who is on the Continent, even after Clevedon told him my father had put me under his protection while he was away."

"I take it your father didn't take kindly to Chatsford's trickery?"

"Not at all. Thanks to Clevedon, he was able to find out just how dire Chatsford's situation was. I was merely a pawn and a means to shore up his depleted coffers."

"I don't think you'll have to worry about Chatsford anymore, Lady Clare," the viscountess said.

"No, she won't," the duchess added. "I imagine Clevedon has given him more than a proper dressing down. My husband will make sure Chatsford won't be able to show his face in the better establishments in London."

"He'll be shunned by his peers," Lady Hertford said. "It couldn't happen to a more deserving man."

Clare finished her brandy and sat back in her chair. "Wexford has asked to court me. He told me he's discussed it with my cousin." She smiled.

"Ah, the evening ends with a silver lining." Lady Hertford beamed.

"Clevedon said he was convinced of his sincerity when Wexford rode nearly nonstop from York to Brighton to make sure you were well. He said not only was that a sign of a concerned gentleman, but of one in love," the duchess added.

The duke was right; Wexford must love her to have raced down from the north of England to be by her side. What was going on? Was she really developing feelings for him as well?

Wexford accepted a brandy from Hertford and stood by the hearth in the viscount's study. Clevedon and two other men were making sure Chatsford left the premises without further incident.

"Hopefully, that'll be the end of Chatsford. I don't imagine he'll show his face for a good while," the viscount remarked.

"I certainly hope so. The man has no scruples."

The door opened and Clevedon walked in. "He's gone."

The viscount picked up another glass and filled it before passing it to Clevedon. "Good riddance, I say."

"Indeed," Clevedon replied.

"He's penniless and desperate. A dangerous combination," Wexford commented.

Clevedon lifted his glass. "Now you can concentrate of courting my cousin. I hope you make it a short courtship."

"That was my intention all along, but now more than ever," Wexford replied. "I thought I would take her on a picnic tomorrow, somewhere secluded."

"There's a place farther down the beach. Not as many people walk there since it's farther from town. There are a couple of places that sit up on a bluff which are easily accessed," Hertford offered. "The viscountess and I still go there when we visit."

"I'll keep that in mind," Wexford said as he downed his brandy.

"I suppose we should rejoin the party. Hopefully, Lady Clare will have recovered from her encounter with Chatsford," Clevedon said.

"Shall we? My wife is serving a buffet, and I believe it's about time for that."

The trio joined the others in the ballroom, where some people were lingering. To one end, tables were filled with all sorts of delicacies to choose from. At the other end, Lady Clare stood with the duchess and several other women.

Wexford looked fondly at Lady Clare. Her silver silk gown shimmered in the candlelight. She gifted him with a smile as she saw him enter the room. The encounter with Chatsford seemed to have had no lasting effect on her other than that she'd had to change gowns. Clare was a strong woman, one who knew what she wanted, and one who would not be deterred by the likes of someone like Chatsford. Other women would suffer from a case of the vapors and have to leave to take to their bed. Not Lady Clare.

"Ladies," he murmured as he bent over her hand. He kissed the back of her glove. "I'm glad to see the incident with Lord Chatsford hasn't ruined your evening."

"I wouldn't give him the satisfaction," she boldly replied.

"Shall we join the others in line for dinner?"

She nodded. "Yes, let's."

Clare turned to the duchess, who, along with the duke, was taking this all in. "You will join us?"

"In a moment. The two of you go ahead," the duchess replied.

Wexford led her across the room to where they waited in a fairly quick moving line. He passed her a plate as they approached the buffet. He watched to see what she might choose. Her choices surprised him as she stayed away from the richer, sauce-laden foods, but insisting he try some of them.

He found a small table which had just been abandoned by two couples who headed outside. Footmen quickly gathered the plates and glasses. She passed one of the footmen her plate and let him place it in front of one of the four chairs.

"This is perfect," she announced as she picked up her fork.

"Yes," he replied. He sat and took a sip of wine.

She thoughtfully took a bite of asparagus, which was paired with a lovely cream sauce. "Do you think we've heard the last of Chatsford?"

"It would behoove him to cry off."

"I'm afraid this incident will follow him for a while. That and the fact that he's destitute," she said.

"That alone will be reason enough for most fathers to hide their daughters from him."

"Well, I'm not worried about him now." She smiled and continued eating. Before Wexford could change the subject, another couple joined them.

12

Two evenings before they were to leave for London, the Duke and Duchess of Clevedon hosted a masked ball. It was to be a small affair, the first ball for the couple since they'd married. Most of the guests were on holiday from their country estates. A few more had made the trip down from London. Bedchambers had been aired out, even though most guests would stay with neighbors or friends.

Rather than costumes, guests would each wear a mask to cover their faces. At precisely midnight, everyone would dispose of their masks to reveal their true identities.

At half past eight, the guests began to trickle in. The ballroom became abuzz with conversation and laughter. Everyone was more daring with a mask on their face. There was an edge of excitement in the room. Conversations grew more risqué.

Wexford craned his neck to get a glimpse of Lady Clare. None of them fit her description or had her ginger hair. Then he turned and saw her. Her mask was covered in a dark green felt and feathers which matched her eyes. Since their picnic the day before, they'd agreed to spend more time with each other, including sharing a few dances at the ball. All day, Wexford found himself anticipating seeing Clare again, and now was not disappointed by her beauty.

He made his way to her and bowed. "Is that you, Lady Clare?"

"Yes, how did you know?"

"I just knew," he murmured.

What was it about wearing a mask? Covering the top of one's face made the bottom more interesting. A person noticed things about others he hadn't before. Like the freckles on her nose and cheeks or how luscious and full her lips were.

The musicians had started playing a lively waltz. "Would you care to dance?"

Her eyes lit up. "Yes, I would."

He led her to the floor. The waltz was in full swing by now, but they quickly found their place. Wexford pressed his hand on her waist, and she moved as he expected. They twirled and spun. It was perfect.

Too quickly, it was over. The music ended, and it took him a minute to release her from his arms and lead her back to the side of the room.

"That was lovely, Wexford."

He bent down. "Parr. You may call me Parr when we're alone. And as you know, no one calls me by my given name. It sounds much too stuffy and old."

"Very well. I'll be sure to remember that."

"Would you care to go outside?"

She nodded slowly. "Yes, it is getting a trifle warm in here."

He led her along the wall to the open doors that led on to the terrace. The surf could be heard in the distance as it crashed along the shoreline. They walked the entire length until they neared the end where there were fewer couples mingling about.

SHE HELD ON TO HIS ARM AS HE LED HER ALONG BY THE HAND. Anticipating what was about to happen sent a shiver down her body. Never before had something felt so right. He was taking her somewhere she might not go if it wasn't with him, but she wanted this opportunity to be with him, to see what was drawing them together.

And then he kissed her. She felt a rush of heat rush through her body as his lips brushed against hers at first. His arms wrapped around her. She sighed against his mouth as their bodies touched. She opened to him as his mouth grew more urgent and the kissed deepened. Her hands held him tighter, resting at where his hair and collar met as his own hands pulled her closer.

The kiss grew deeper as the heat between them thrived.

Too soon, he ended the kiss. "Clare," he whispered.

He nipped at her earlobe. She moaned. She wanted him to touch her. She wanted to touch him. She'd been dreaming of nothing else since their lovely but chaste picnic under the watchful eyes of her maid and his groom.

He groaned as she moved her hands through his hair. His lips moved down her neck, his teeth nibbling on her, raining fire along her skin.

"I want you, my darling. May I come to you later?"

"Yes," she whispered. "Yes."

His hand wandered to her breast, where he cupped it while his other hand held her face as he kissed her deeply, as though his very existence depended on it. She felt on fire as they devoured each other. Clare didn't want this moment to end.

Moments later, Wexford pulled away from her. They stood in a comfortable silence as he regained his wits. "You look like a goddess in that gown. The minutes couldn't pass quickly enough for me today until I could hold you in my arms again."

"Thank you. You are quite handsome yourself this evening."

"Come," he murmured. "We should go back or even indoors before someone notices we're missing."

"I don't care what anyone thinks" she replied breathlessly. "However, being that this is my cousin and his wife's first ball, I shall yield."

He laughed. "That's one of the things I love about you, Clare. You're bolder than any woman I know. I like it."

She gave him a flirtatious wink. "Good, because I don't intend to stop just because you're courting me."

"I wouldn't expect you too. Ever. You've got passion."

———

WEXFORD QUIETLY WALKED DOWN THE HALLWAY UNTIL HE came to Clare's room. Slowly he turned the knob. He opened it far enough to fit his body through the opening, thankful the door hadn't squeaked. He shut it behind him, then took the time to get his bearings.

The room was dark, with a hint of moonlight filtering in around the heavy drapes. He waited for his eyes to adjust. He could make out various pieces of furniture in the room. Then he came across the bed.

She lay there like an angel, the sheets mussed around her, one arm flung over her head, covering her ginger hair.

She slowly moved, most likely dreaming. Then her eyes opened as if she'd sensed him there, and she met his gaze.

"Wexford?" she whispered. "You finally came."

"It took me longer than I expected," he whispered.

She sat up, swinging her legs over the side of the bed. They faced each other as he took her hands in his.

"I love you," he said. "We belong together."

"I love you too," she whispered as he pulled her to him, their fingers entwined.

"Clare," he whispered. "Let me make love to you."

She nodded. "Kiss me."

He sucked in a ragged breath. When he did speak, his voice was deep and rough. "Clare."

The only sound was the rustle of his clothing as he removed it, allowing it to drop to the floor. He closed the distance between them and quickly unbuttoned her dress, then unlaced her corset and removed the remainder of her clothing. She crawled up on the bed and waited on him.

He joined her under the sheet. He traced her bottom lip with one finger. His lips found the hollow in the base of her neck. "So lovely," he whispered.

He didn't look at her when he spoke. His fingers continued to follow the curvature of her shoulders down to her breasts. Her nipple hardened as his thumb circled it before his lips covered her breast and sucked. She held on to him, not wanting him to stop. Ever.

She reached over and placed a hand on one side of his jaw. His whiskers were rough.

He pulled her closer and ran his hand over the curve of her hip and buttocks. He nuzzled his way down. She could feel his arousal against her thigh.

She was completely vulnerable to him, completely open to him.

He kissed her again. This time, there was need in his kiss as his hand slid to that place between her legs and teased her. She was moist. Her legs parted, beckoning him.

His fingers slid inside her, exploring her. This felt so good, but it wasn't enough. She had a need only he could relieve.

He covered her with his body as she wrapped her arms around his shoulders. A pressure was building inside her, and then a sharp sensation swept through her as he broke through her maidenhead. All she could do was hold on to him as a restlessness flowed through her.

He made love to her gently, until her body responded and she crested a glorious peak. Within moments, he gasped and softly called out her name with his release, which came upon him before he'd been able to withdraw.

He held her, whispering words of love. He wanted her unconditionally, all of her. He also realized how selfish he'd been. A child might come from this one night. Not that it would be the last night, but he had let his emotions and his lust overtake him.

Wexford found himself falling asleep. "I need to leave, before the servants stir."

"Must you? I rather like this."

He kissed her forehead. "As do I, but I'm afraid I must."

He let her go, sat up and swung his legs over the side of the bed. She watched him as he began to dress. It was the first time she'd ever truly seen a man naked, and Wexford was a rather remarkable specimen. He was muscular from all the time he spent outdoors.

"I'll see you at breakfast?" she inquired.

"Yes. Clevedon and I have an appointment late morning, and we thought you and the duchess might like to join us.

You could shop while we're at our meeting. Afterward, we could have lunch together."

She smiled. "I'd much rather spend time alone with you, sir."

"And we will. I thought we could take a carriage ride to see some of the countryside, if it's not too late, and your cousin agrees."

"I look forward to it, and I'll see you at breakfast. Now go, before we get caught."

Wexford leaned down and brushed a kiss on her lips. He turned, opened the door, and disappeared.

Clare fell against the pillows and let out a sigh. Before she could think about the time she'd just spent with Wexford, she fell asleep, only to be awakened by the sound of her maid throwing open the draperies.

"Good morning, my lady. It's a beautiful day. I have the tub filled with hot water for you to bathe."

"Very well, and I believe I'd like to wear that new dove-gray dress."

Her maid smiled. "I've readied it for you, my lady."

Clare wrapped her robe around her as something caught her eye. Blood on the sheet. It wasn't a concern. Her courses had never been regular, so her maid would think nothing of it.

She entered the bathing chamber, climbed into the steaming tub, and sank back. Grabbing the linen cloth, she then picked up the cake of lavender soap her maid had placed on a small stool situated next to the tub.

The water felt heavenly against her skin, and if she had more time, she would dally. Breakfast would be served shortly, and she longed to see Wexford. He was magnificent in so many ways. How long would their courtship last? She was not fond of the fact that men controlled such matters.

Perhaps she would bring up the matter on their carriage ride later today. She knew her mother in particular would want a grand wedding, and she'd probably want it held at the family estate in Scotland. Summer was so fleeting in Scotland, there might not be time to plan a summer wedding in the gardens. No, it would have to be an indoor affair. No matter, Wexford still had to ask her to marry him. Since they'd only just started courting, a wedding could be a while, which was exactly why she intended to speak frankly with him today.

A short time later, she was looking at herself in the mirror one last time. Her maid had gotten every hair in place and the dress fit perfectly, needing no adjustments as gowns sometimes did at the last minute. All that was left was for her to join the others in the breakfast room.

She descended the stairs, sun shining in through the windows, and joined the duke and duchess where they sat talking in the breakfast room. Wexford sat at the other end, buttering a piece of toast. He looked dashing, recently shaved and bathed. The suit he wore was a deep gray with a lavender waistcoat and crisp white shirt and cravat.

The men immediately stood as she entered the room. She sat where she usually did, across from the duchess and to the left of her cousin.

"Good morning," she said cheerfully.

Everyone mumbled their greetings, but Wexford had a hint of a smile on his face, the rake. But he was her rake and she wouldn't change him for love nor money.

She smiled as the footman brought her a plate. She picked up a piece of toast and began to slather orange marmalade on it.

"I thought we'd look in Mrs. Godfrey's shop while we're in town. I understand she carries some of the finest lace in all of England," the duchess said, picking up her teacup.

"I heard my mother say that once. She said Mrs. Godfrey makes two trips a year to procure the best."

"I should like to purchase that and a pair or two of the kid gloves she sells. There are none softer outside London, I'm told," the duchess continued.

Clare bit into her toast. The marmalade was divine, some of the best she'd tasted. Everything had a better flavor today. She wondered if it had something to do with Wexford and the time they'd spent together the night before. She gazed at him through her lashes and caught him doing the same.

She found herself wanting more of him. She wanted him to show her the ways of making love. Last night, he had been gentle, knowing it was her first time. Today, she lusted after him, wanting him to touch her everywhere, but especially in those places once forbidden.

"I think the ball was a success, don't you?" the duchess asked Clare.

"Everyone seemed to enjoy themselves."

Far different from the stifling ballrooms of London. "Yes, and I have you to thank for suggesting using the terrace. It's something that won't soon be forgotten."

"My mother always told me you have to take chances and do daring things to get noticed by society," Clare replied.

"I certainly believe that was the case last night."

The gentlemen excused themselves, stating something about business and that they'd all meet up within the house later to head toward town.

The duchess smiled after the men left. "You must tell me what is going on between you and Wexford."

"Whatever do you mean?" she asked demurely.

"You spent a great deal of time together last evening. This morning, you're both smiling and stealing glances at one another."

"Clevedon did give his permission for us to court, so I suppose whatever you think you've seen may have something to do with that," she replied slyly.

"Yes, the duke told me. He thinks Wexford will make you an excellent husband."

"My cousin's eager to marry me off, I see."

"No, but he does think Wexford is a suitable match and knows your father would approve."

"Speaking of my father, do we know when he and my mother might return? I so rarely hear from either of them."

"Probably because they're traveling," the duchess replied.

"If this were to turn into something more, how long would we have to wait until they returned?"

"That's something to discuss with Clevedon."

Clare shook her head. "I wouldn't want a long betrothal."

"Whyever not?"

"I really detest the thought of a grand wedding with hundreds of people attending, most of whom I'd barely know. I'd much rather have something small and more intimate."

"I understand. If you'd like, I can speak with the duke about your parents' plans. It would be better coming from me. He might suspect you're up to something if you start to inquire."

"What? I can't inquire about my own parents and their impending return?"

The duchess smiled sweetly. "Of course you can, but you know as well as I do you are sometimes not discreet."

"True. I might just blurt something out before poor Wexford's even had a chance to discuss marriage with my cousin."

"Good, I'm glad we agree on that. I suggest we come up with a couple of possibilities for when he does offer for you."

"Yes. With or without my parents, and where?"

"Patience, Clare. Patience."

"I know, but it's so hard to be."

And you think Wexford's the one?"

Clare nodded. "Oh yes. He owns a piece of my heart. He's the only man I wish to marry."

"Then I'm happy for you. Things will work out. You'll see."

Clare pushed back from the table. "I suppose we should quit chattering and finish getting ready. I know how my cousin hates to be kept waiting."

Wexford took her hand and led her in the direction of the beach that ran in front of Brighton. They were at the far end, where people seldom gathered. Too far away from town and everything that went on around the shoreline there.

There were a couple of small old row boats that sat abandoned next to a fishing shack, the opening the farthest from civilization.

"Once the fishermen have returned for the day, no one comes here, Clare. We're quite safe from prying eyes. Do you trust me?

"Yes, Parr, and I want you."

He then picked Clare up and placed her voluptuous bottom on an abandoned boat next to the door of the fishing shack. He placed his hands on her knees and pulled them apart in a slow, methodical motion, watching her face.

Clare's cheeks darkened, and she licked her lips, causing him to groan.

He bent his head, and they kissed as if they'd been kissing for years. Her mouth opened instantly, and her fingers entwined in his hair. His hands moved down to grip her hips.

Finally, he pulled away, her mouth a deep red, bruised from his kisses. Her eyes were heavy with lust. He placed one hand under her skirts, his fingers caressing her private places. She clenched his forearms, and her mouth opened, but no sound emerged.

Wexford kissed her on her left cheekbone and then once again her mouth.

"Do you like this?" he whispered.

A pleading sound emerged from her throat. She buried her face in his waistcoat as he bent over her and he stroked her with callused fingers. He pushed one finger, then a second into her, past plump, swollen flesh.

She cried out as an orgasm slammed into her, and she shuddered.

"You're mine, Clare," Wexford said, his voice reassuring.

She was vaguely aware of him tearing open his breeches. His hands came around her hips, and he thrust forward. Clare curled her legs around his hips to pull him closer. He entered her in one smooth stroke, her passage wet for him.

Her mouth sought his and she whimpered his name as he rocked into her, thrusting so hard, she thought she might split apart. There was no pain, just fullness. Pleasure shot through her in waves as Wexford braced his hands at her sides, his hips grinding into her. His face had a look of ferocious severity as he lost himself in her.

He groaned and slammed into her as an orgasm flew through her from head to toe, where only the two of them were allowed.

His body shuddered again and again as he came. He jerked forward, shouting out her name.

When they'd both recovered, Wexford stood and made

himself somewhat presentable. Her hair hadn't survived well during their tryst. "Your hair looks nice down."

She stood and he wound his arms around her from behind. "I love the way you smell after we've made love."

"We best be careful, or I'll be with child before you know it."

"Would that be so terrible?"

She cocked her head curiously. "Do you want to?"

"No. There's nothing I love better than to feel my seed flood you. If a child comes from our love, we'll deal with it. I want to marry you, Clare."

He pulled her into his arms before she had time to respond as he ravished her mouth with a kiss.

"Wexford! Yes! Yes I'll marry you!"

"Parr, I told you, you may call me Parr when we're alone," he said. He smiled. "Do you know I've had a cock-stand all morning waiting for this, for this afternoon, to be alone with you?"

"Very well. Parr. We must start back. Someone will notice."

"To hell with what people think," he said.

She picked up her hat and began placing it back on her head. "Not changing the subject, but there is much to discuss."

"Such as?" he asked with a mischievous grin.

"How long a courtship you plan for us to have. You know, things that really aren't discussed with the woman."

"Things have already gone past simple courting."

She nodded. "Agreed. I would prefer our courtship is short. I feel we both know what we want, and that is to marry."

"I care a great deal for you, Clare. In fact, I find I've fallen madly in love you, and I promise you our courtship will be a short one."

They began to walk back to the carriage. The wind had picked up, and dark clouds were rolling in from the ocean. A storm was not far behind.

"I know you have your townhouse in London, but where do you call home, where is your ancestral seat?" she asked.

"Wexford castle. It's outside of Stratford"

"Shakespeare's birthplace," she said.

"Yes. The castle is undergoing some extensive renovations at the present time."

"Such as?"

"Adding water closets and bathing chambers. Running water, new paint, and wall coverings," he replied. "I don't think it'd been touched in several generations."

They reached the carriage, and Wexford handed her in just as the rain began to come down in torrents.

They both laughed.

"Is the earldom self-sufficient?"

"Not completely. I have outside business interests. Some, my father or grandfather started. I'm considering investing in a canal."

"I've seen a few. Are they for moving goods more quickly, as on a river?" she inquired.

He nodded. "Yes, but rivers don't always flow where the goods must go. Canals can go and carry heavier goods that a carriage or wagon would have problems with."

"That makes sense."

The rain continued to pelt down around them, the skies so black, there was no doubt the rain was there to stay for the remainder of the day.

"I've thoroughly enjoyed today," he said. He sat across

from her, watching her as she peered out the carriage window.

"Since there's nothing planned for this evening, perhaps we can all play cards," she said.

"Or cribbage."

"I'm not very good."

"Excellent, it gives me a chance to beat you at something," he replied, grinning.

"It's a good thing there's not a billiards table in the house."

"Why's that?"

"Because I would beat both you and Clevedon without blinking twice."

"That good, eh?"

"Yes, my father taught me when I was much younger, and now he won't even play me. Says I'm too good."

"Wait until I take you to Wexford Castle. There's an entire room devoted to billiards. We'll just see how good you are."

She laughed. "Promises, promises."

It was a week later. Wexford had arrived at his townhouse in London the night before in the pouring rain and winds. Clevedon and the duchess had followed in the duke's new traveling carriage. Clare had traveled with him with the duke's permission as far as the outskirts of London, making the journey considerably more tolerable.

He left her with her cousin, with plans for the four of them to attend a special performance of *Othello*. Until then, Wexford's day would be filled with business meetings and the like. First, he had to go over his own correspondence and the ledgers his man of business had left for him to read and approve. It was still raining outside, with no sign of it letting up any time soon.

Finishing breakfast, Wexford made his way to his study. Sitting on the middle of the desk was a missive from Clevedon. He sat down and opened it, reading it twice.

Clevedon had received word from Clare's father that they were about to leave Paris to return to Scotland. The letter Clevedon had written to the duke hadn't made it to him when this latest was sent.

He wished to see Clevedon at his estate to hear about what prospects, if any, Clare might have. Clevedon indicated they would be leaving for his Scottish estate in two days' time. Telling Wexford it would be a good idea for him to join them, he suggested they meet for lunch today to go over the details. "Details" meaning the matter of Clare's father.

He knew from what Clevedon had told him that MacDougal was not an easy man to get along with, especially if you weren't Scottish. If Wexford joined them and MacDougal met him, he would quickly change his mind. He wanted to see his daughter married, and preferred it was to someone she loved. He didn't want to be put in the situation of having to choose a husband for his sharp-tongued daughter.

He put the note aside and went through the rest of his correspondence. Invitations, mainly, and one regarding the venture of digging a canal he was interested in investing in.

Wexford found he couldn't concentrate on any of it; his mind kept wandering back to Clare. Her parents' return was going to change things. They needed to have everything finalized between them before they left for Clevedon's Scottish home. That way, they could plan a wedding and marry before returning to London or the castle if the renovations were finished.

A number of hours later, he walked into White's, where he found Clevedon waiting for him, reading a newspaper.

"It seems we have a good deal to discuss," Wexford said as he sat in a leather chair across from the duke.

"Yes. I was surprised to hear from MacDougal. I hadn't expected them to return for another month."

"Does Clare know her parents are returning earlier than planned?"

He nodded. "Yes. She's voiced concern already about where this leaves the two of you."

Wexford chuckled at the thought. He had to give her credit, she always thought through each and every obstacle that was thrown her way.

"I can just imagine her pacing the floor and having a few choice words to say about her parents' early arrival."

"That's why I thought we could discuss just that. Away from the house, away from Clare."

"And just what would you be wanting to discuss?" Wexford asked arching a brow.

"Are you going to ask Clare to marry you now, or are you going to await until she's in Scotland with her family?"

"I've already asked her to marry me, and she's said yes. I'm very happy, but of course, we need her father's permission."

Clevedon placed the newspaper on a table beside him and stretched his legs. "It's imperative you speak to her father as quickly as possible because Chatsford hasn't given up. The duke mentioned that if Clare wasn't betrothed by the time he and the duchess arrived home, he would give Chatsford permission to marry her."

"Really? MacDougal obviously hasn't gotten all of your

correspondence. I can't allow that to happen," he said. "What do you suggest?"

"If you truly want to marry my cousin, we need to act quickly. The duke gave me permission to act on his behalf in any marriage negotiations regarding her dowry. You and I can go over that and finalize it before we leave."

"You know I want nothing more than to marry Clare," he replied. "I'm sure when her father sees how happy we are, he'll give his permission."

"Chatsford has left London. My best guess is he's headed to Scotland to be there when MacDougal arrives. By the time we arrive, the marriage contract will be settled and Clare will be expected to marry the man."

"I thought we'd seen the last of him," Wexford hissed.

"Obviously, we didn't give the man enough credit regarding the ends he would go to get what he wants."

"So what now?"

Clevedon leaned back in his chair, his fingers steepled, and smiled. "I suggest you and Clare marry in Gretna Green. The duchess and I will go with you to serve as your witnesses. I keep a townhome in Edinburgh. I thought the two of you could stay in town for about a week while the duchess and I return home and inform the duke of what's transpired."

"Then I suggest we have lunch, and afterward, we can discuss the marriage details."

By the time they finished their steaks, the details had been worked out. All that was left was to meet with the solicitors and sign the documents.

"Why don't you come early, before we leave for the theater. We can discuss all this with Clare."

"She's not going to be happy about one thing," Wexford said.

"What's that?"

"That I've never formally asked for her hand. She says it doesn't matter, but every girl wants her father's approval. Plus there's the matter of her dowry, and he would expect me to do the honorable thing."

"You can still do that. I just want her to understand what might happen if the two of you wait. There's really no time to get word to the duke, and by the time he would get it, Chatsford would be in Scotland."

"When you put it to her like that, she'll understand."

14

Clevedon stood in front of James MacDougal, Duke of Renfrew, in the duke's drawing room ten days later to explain to Clare's father that she was in love and had married the Earl of Wexford two days prior.

Upon hearing the news, the duke appeared angry that his nephew had allowed them to marry in Gretna Green rather than have the large wedding his wife, the duchess, had always dreamed of for her daughter. Once Clevedon explained Clare's fears about Chatsford and some of the man's misdeeds and misrepresentations, however, MacDougal relaxed. But not for long once he realized he'd been tricked by Chatsford.

"I cannot believe I welcomed that scoundrel into my home."

"He's quite well-schooled in the art of deception," Clevedon replied.

"He presented himself as a gentleman. We even went over Clare's dowry. He said he was in love with my daughter."

Clevedon cocked a brow. "Where is he staying?"

"Here. I saw no reason for him to stay in town. I thought he'd like to spend time with Clare, and that she could show him around."

"Clare and Wexford will arrive in five days. Chatsford needs to be gone before they return."

MacDougal nodded. "Agreed. Neither of them need to return with Chatsford still here. I'll take care of the matter myself."

"Are you sure? I had enough dealings with the man. I'd be happy to be present when you do."

"I suppose you're right. I know nothing of the man's true background. Stay and we can take care of the problem today."

"You said he was here?"

"Yes, I believe he was taking care of some correspondence in the library."

More than likely, Chatsford was writing creditors to inform them of his upcoming nuptials and assure them they would be paid. Men like him never changed. He would always be scheming up the next great deception.

Clevedon followed his uncle to the library. Seated at a writing desk at one end of the room was Chatsford. He looked up from his correspondence and smiled broadly at Clevedon.

"Your Grace, how good to see you. Have you brought my bride with you?"

"No, I'm afraid not. Lady Clare and the Earl of Wexford were married in Gretna Green. They're enjoying some time alone before they return."

Chatsford sat bolt upright, his eyebrows shooting to his hairline. "Married? Why on earth would Clare marry Wexford when she and I had an arrangement?"

Clevedon stepped closer. "I'll ask you not to call my

cousin by her given name. As for your 'arrangement,' you know as well as I there is no arrangement. I thought I made that abundantly clear in Brighton."

"Has *Lady* Clare told her new husband that she carries my child?" he asked smugly.

"Another lie," MacDougal said.

"I'm afraid neither of you knows her well at all. After the incident in Brighton, we began meeting late at night. We consummated our relationship, and that resulted in a child."

"If this were true," Clevedon spoke, "Clare wouldn't even know she carries a child yet."

"It's just another lie," MacDougal said quietly. "I want you to pack your things and leave my home. You are no longer welcome, my lord."

"But...but...but, Your Grace, you're not really going to believe this, are you? He doesn't know what's best for your daughter."

"I've known Clevedon since the day he was born, and I trust him implicitly."

Chatsford wasn't about to give up that easily, and kept pleading. "What about what Lady Clare wants?"

"I can assure you she's with the man she loves and wants to spend the rest of her life with," Clevedon said. "Now may I suggest you go pack your things and be on your way like the duke asked you? Before we have the footmen show you the door."

Chatsford picked up the paper he'd been writing on, wadded it into a ball, and tossed it into the fireplace. For the first time, Clevedon could actually say the man looked defeated. He'd thought that by going directly to Lady Clare's father, he could convince him that he and the duke's daughter were in love, and therefore have everything agreed upon and the dowry his.

Luckily, MacDougal was not so easily convinced. Not only did he need to hear from his daughter that she wanted to marry this man, but he depended on Clevedon's wisdom.

MacDougal followed Chatsford's retreating figure as they showed him out of the library and to the grand hall, making sure he heeded his words that Chatsford was unwelcome in his home.

"You know I wouldn't have finalized anything until I heard from Clare."

"Yes, sir."

"I suppose I need to tell the duchess her daughter's married, and why she went to Gretna Green. She's going to be disappointed, you know."

"Aye, I know. At the time, it seemed like the safest and most logical way to handle the Chatsford situation. Clare's happy. That's all that's important."

MacDougal nodded, running a hand through his silver hair. "Care to join me in a wee dram? To celebrate and for me to garner the courage to tell my wife."

"I'd be honored to, Uncle. I think you'll find Wexford to your liking...for an Englishman."

The two men laughed and then enjoyed a dram of whiskey.

WEXFORD AND CLARE RETURNED TO CLEVEDON'S TOWNHOUSE in Edinburgh after a day of shopping, sightseeing, and having lunch. It was the first time they'd been out of the house, or rather out of their bedchamber, since arriving from Gretna Green.

Though Clare was thoroughly enjoying getting to know

her husband better, she longed for the day they would leave Scotland and travel to his country home.

Wexford seemed to be just as restless as she was. She knew he had business to attend to, and though he would never begrudge her this time together, he was anxious to return as well.

First, however, they would have to go visit her parents and introduce them to Wexford. She knew her mother and father were anxious to meet the man their daughter had chosen for a husband, and she was excited for him to meet them as well.

Their wedding night in Gretna Green had not been fulfilled, as Wexford found an inn a most inappropriate place to consummate their marriage. Instead, they waited until the next evening, once they were safely tucked away in the duke's home in Edinburgh.

Until today, they rarely left the bedchamber, even taking meals in the suite. Clare knew this would likely be the last time for many weeks she would truly be alone with her husband without the demands of life. He had business to attend to, and once they arrived at his castle near Stafford, Parr would have estate business to take up his time.

"Are you excited to see your mother and father?" Parr asked as he closed the door to the bedchamber.

They had returned from their day out, and footmen had deposited his wife's purchases on and near a small table in the bedchamber's sitting room.

"Yes, my father especially. We've always been close. My mother, on the other hand, is quite a different story."

He strode over to a nearby table and poured them both a small glass of claret. "You don't get along with your mother?"

"My mother is of the old school. Women are to be

submissive to their husbands and take care of the household and children. I, on the other hand...well, you know
how I am. Needless to say, my mother and I clash quite a
bit."

He took a sip of claret and pondered what his bride had
just told him. "Surely there must be something the two of
you can agree on?"

"Oh yes, but even that can change daily," Clare replied.
She began to unwrap a package containing some fripperies
she'd purchased. "I imagine she'll want to hold some sort of
party now that we've married."

"Clevedon warned me of that."

She smiled up at him. "Then you're agreeable to the
idea?"

"I don't see where I have any other choice. Besides, it
would be rude if we didn't allow her and your father to
introduce us to their friends."

"Yes, it would. Especially in my mother's eyes," she
replied.

"I'm quite interested to see Clevedon's horses as well."

"Yes, I thought you would like to see his breeding
operation."

Clare was anxious as well. The duchess had confided in
her that she was with child, but was waiting for just the
right moment to tell Clevedon. Clare knew if she were
correct in her own calculations, their child would have a
cousin born just afterward.

"...you haven't heard a word I've said, Clare."

She gazed at him. "I'm sorry."

"I understand. This has all been a lot to take in. Gretna
Green, staying here, and then we have the trip to the castle
to look forward to."

"Yes."

"I thought we'd leave tomorrow for your family home," he announced.

"So soon?" she asked, then added, "Never mind, you do have business matters which require your attention."

He cupped her face with one hand, his callused finger stroking her cheek. "I promise I'll make it up to you, wife."

"I know you will. There is something else I'd like to discuss with you."

He arched a brow and dropped his hand. "What's that?"

"I should wait to tell you this, but I find I cannot."

"Go on..."

She bit her lip and folder her hands over her middle. "I believe I'm with child, Parr. By my calculations and the fact I'm late with my monthly courses, I have to say this happened the first time we made love in Brighton."

The corners of his mouth turned up. "You're sure? That is marvelous."

"Fairly sure. I'd like to keep this between us for now. Until I'm certain," she replied. "I wouldn't have told you yet, but I was too excited at the thought."

Parr pulled her close to him, bent his head, and kissed her. "I'm so glad you decided to tell me. I won't utter a word until you tell me I may."

"Thank you."

"What about your parents?"

Clare pursed her lips. "You'll soon find out that my mother can be somewhat of a prude. Especially when it comes to me. She expects me to be perfect."

"Then we won't tell them. Not yet. You can write them a letter when you're ready for them to know."

"Thank you."

Wexford kissed her again. His hands found their way to her hair, and his fingers began to pull hairpins out, letting her ginger hair flow down her back. He trailed kisses on her face and down her throat. She'd worn the orange blossoms and honey scent he loved. His hands cupped her bottom as he carried her across the room to the bed. He deposited her at the edge and pulled up her skirts. She noted his surprise to find she wore no undergarments in order to tease him or in anticipation of some naughty lovemaking in the carriage or now, alone in their bedchamber in the middle of the afternoon.

15

Clare's parents, the Duke and Duchess of Renfrew, were sitting in the red-and-gold drawing room when she and Wexford arrived that afternoon. Surprisingly, both her parents greeted her warmly and welcomed her new husband into the family. Clare had been wary of what to expect from them.

On one hand, they'd left her in Clevedon's protection while they holidayed on the Continent, which included accepting a suitable marriage proposal. They hadn't expected her to go as far as marrying in Gretna Green. Now they could tell their side of things.

"Tea?" her mother asked as she immediately signaled a nearby footman for a fresh tray.

"Please," Clare replied. She and Wexford sat on a gold settee across from her parents. Niceties aside, Clare waited for the inquisition to begin. It was what she called it when her parents wanted answers or scolded her for some minor infraction.

Finally, her mother spoke. "Why Gretna Green, Clare? Why?"

"Because it was necessary, as I'm sure my cousin has already explained to Papa."

Her father spoke up in her defense. "I told you why. Clare and Wexford seem quite happy, so no harm has been done."

The duchess threw her husband a look that an outsider might interpret as a request for him to shut up.

"No harm has been done?" the duchess trilled. "She has always had you wrapped around her little finger. You've always sided with her."

The duke chose to ignore his wife's biting comments and turned to Wexford. "I understand your family seat is near Stafford. Lovely area. Is that where you and Clare will live?"

Wexford nodded just as the same footman returned with a fresh tray. He waited for the young man to finish his task.

"Yes, I thought we'd stay a fortnight at Wexford Castle before traveling to my family's home in London. I have business I need to finish there."

The duke nodded. "Yes, I understand from Clevedon you're researching building a canal."

Before Wexford could answer his father-in-law, the duchess chimed in. "You will be staying here for at least a fortnight before you return to England."

"Mama, you cannot expect my husband to stay away from his businesses and estates much longer."

The duchess sternly eyed her daughter and new son-in-law. "The duke and I will be hosting a ball to celebrate your marriage. You will allow me this much since you eloped to Gretna Green."

Wexford realized this was going to be a game of wills with the duchess, and the best way to handle her was to let her think she was getting her own way.

"We would be honored, but I'm afraid we won't be able

to stay longer than a fortnight. I cannot be away from my responsibilities much longer."

It wasn't a complete lie. He had people who ran Wexford Castle and its land with years of expertise. His land and estate manager was one of the best. All he had to do was send a letter explaining the cause of the delay, and the man would proceed as he always had.

The duchess poured tea for everyone and passed the cups. "Excellent. It'll give you and the duke time to get to know each other and discuss matters better suited to men." She took a sip of tea, gazing at Clare over her teacup. "You and I have much to discuss. We'll plan to hold the ball two weeks from Thursday."

"As you wish," she replied. She was avoiding conflict with the duchess by agreeing to what she wanted. She took a sip of tea and stared at her mother. She certainly hoped she wouldn't become like her, that she would be more caring and encouraging of her own children.

Wexford was right. The news of her pregnancy would have to wait. News such as this so soon would surely send her mother to her bed. The duchess seemed to view sex as a duty. She bore her husband children, nothing more. She didn't enjoy the act because women of her station weren't supposed to.

"Come," her mother said. "We have a great many invitations to write. There is time for us to begin before we must dress for dinner. Your father can show Wexford around or discuss whatever it is men talk about."

"Mother, we just arrived. Can't we begin in the morning?"

"Don't be ridiculous," she snapped. "I'll meet you in the breakfast room. The light is so much better there. Fifteen minutes, Clare." Her mother rose and nodded to Wexford before quitting the room.

Clare sighed and finished her tea before setting the cup down on a table. "I see some things never change."

"No, but she'll come around. Right now, she is in shock," her father said.

"You mean dismayed because she didn't get to have the grand wedding she's always wanted me to have."

The duke chuckled. "You know your mother far too well."

"If you gentlemen will excuse me, I think I will freshen up before Mother ties me to the table." She turned to the duke. "Papa, Wexford has a great interest in well-bred horses. Why don't you take him to the stables?"

She patted her husband's knee before standing. "I'll see you in a couple of hours. You'll be having a far better time than I shall. Remember that."

Clare left the room and went through the great hall to the grand staircase at the other side of the room. Her grandfather had done some extensive renovations to the castle since it was no longer used as it once was. The grand hall was no longer a place for clan and friends to gather for a meal. No, he tried to turn it into a fine country estate where the lord and lady of the castle hosted their friends and family in an elaborate dining room.

She walked to the top of the stairs and headed in the direction of her old rooms. One of the chambermaids stopped her.

"Your mother had your and your husband's bags put in the yellow bedchamber, my lady."

A guest room, not a bedchamber in the family section. It was down another hall, away from the family. It shouldn't have surprised her, though she was unsure whether her mother was doing it to punish her or because her rooms might not be considered good enough for newlyweds. Clare shook her head. No, she was being punished.

"Thank you," she replied and turned toward the guest hallway.

She found the duchess in the breakfast room ordering her lady's maid, Etta, and anyone else who happened to cross her path to do her bidding. To one side sat a stack of cream paper stock. Nearby, pens and ink and other miscellaneous items were waiting.

Clare neared the table and smiled faintly at the sight of a note her mother had written out with the exact instructions she wanted followed.

"Don't just stand around, Clare. We have hundreds of invitations to write by the end of tomorrow."

"Hundreds? Who are you inviting at such short notice, Mother?" She sat across from where she knew her mother would sit.

"Friends and acquaintances close by, in Edinburgh and London. A scattering will be sent to people we know in England as well." The duchess sat, picked up her pen, and began to write on the paper in front of her.

"I don't know why you can't do something smaller this time. Wait until next spring to hold such a grand affair."

"No, we cannot," the duchess said sternly. "You ran off to Gretna Green, of all places. No, it's you who owes us. You shall dress up in one of your finest ball gowns and you will smile, be polite, and converse with the guests. Now let's stop talking and start writing."

Clare picked up a pen and began writing. She knew her other friends' mothers were not nearly as strict or demanding. They appeared to be the exact opposite of her own mother.

Clearly, her mother had her favorite, and it wasn't her. That honor belonged to her brother, Charles. He could never do any wrong in her mother's eyes, regardless of the mischief he might have gotten into, either at home or at school.

Her mother thought Charles required a wife. He needed someone to give him heirs to keep the dukedom alive and well. If her parents only knew he'd married already. She wondered how they would take to the news. Charles had sworn her to secrecy, and she had agreed. They had been close as children, but after Charles was sent off to school, that all changed.

"It's too bad Charles can't be here," Clare said.

"Yes, it is," the duchess responded.

Clare set aside a finished invitation and started on another. "Has either of them found someone suitable to marry?"

Her mother sat ramrod straight in her chair and smiled. "You haven't heard? Dugan is to marry the Earl of Argyll's daughter. All the arrangements have been worked out."

Clare all but sputtered, "Dugan? In an arranged marriage? That's so unlike him. I certainly hope this chit's dowry is huge and she is pleasant to look at."

"Your father and I decided this was what was best for him. It will unite two well-bred families."

She stopped her work and forced a smile. "When will the blessed event happen?"

"Late next spring, if all goes according to plan."

Of course it would. Her mother would have it no other way.

"I'm glad for him. Truly I am," she replied. She'd always been cautious where Dugan was concerned. Her cousin was known to take advantage of people and situations, making her wonder if that's not what he was doing now. "What is her name?"

"Grizela Campbell. I believe she was named after her paternal grandmother."

"That is a very old Gaelic name, one you don't hear used frequently anymore."

Her mother beamed as she finished another invitation and set it aside. "Yes, I suppose it is."

"How old is Grizela?"

"My, so many questions," the duchess replied.

"I simply want to know something about my cousin's probable wife before I meet her."

"Very well. I believe Grizela is eight and ten."

That was certainly an age gap, almost ten years, and Clare would bet she was a dewy-eyed debutante who had only seen the world as presented by her parents. Her mother was going to be in for a shock when Charles returned with his native bride.

An hour or two went by, the invitations were made, and her mother and she grew silent the way they usually did. Her mother seemed to have no interest in knowing about Wexford or her trip to Brighton, the things a mother might want her daughter to share with her.

Then it was time to dress for dinner. Clare hurried up the stairs to the rooms she and Wexford would share.

She found Wexford comfortably seated by the hearth enjoying a whiskey. Upon seeing her, he immediately stood and crossed the room. "You look like you could use this more than I." He handed her the glass, kissing her on the forehead.

"Thank you, and yes, I need something in order to calm me after spending time with my mother. She is so impossible to be around."

Wexford poured himself a whiskey from the sideboard as he listened to Clare share the past couple of hours with her mother.

"Did you know my cousin Dugan is betrothed to Lady Grizela Campbell? Her father is the Duke of Argyll, a very powerful man."

"You aren't happy for your him, sweet?"

"Yes, of course I am. It's just that he does nothing unless it benefits him. And there's the matter of Charles and his foreign-bred wife."

She drank a long sip and sat before the fire. Wexford joined her. "It's obvious your mother and you have a strained relationship. Surely you can muddle through. We'll plan on leaving the day after this party your mother's so intent on giving."

"Mother's never hidden the fact I've been a disappointment to her. Her focus has always been on how perfect Charles and Dugan are, and now dotes on his bride-to-be," she said. "Did you know she is nothing more than a girl? There's at least ten years' difference in age between them. I can't imagine Dugan being happy."

"Well, from what your father says, it's an arranged marriage."

She looked at him curiously. "You and Papa discussed Dugan's upcoming marriage?"

Wexford sat next to her. "Yes, my dove. Is that so hard to believe? Your father and I seemed to get along quite well."

"No, I suppose given my relationship with my mother, I never expected Papa would be won over so easily."

He waggled his eyebrows. "Well, I'm told I'm the man all fathers wish their daughters would meet and marry."

"Really? How so?" she teased.

"I never divulge my secrets."

lowed them to sit directly alongside each other was
her when she and Wexford were placed across from
other.

rizela has a wonderful idea," Dugan announced.
you're having a ball for Clare and Wexford, Grizela
sted we announce our upcoming nuptials then. We'll
again, of course, at her father and mother's ball, but
everyone will be here, why not?"

Why not indeed. Clare was seething at the very thought.
was her and Wexford's one time to celebrate the
iest event in their lives. Now, that scheming little tart
already figured out how to turn it around and make it
t her and Dugan.

Her cousin had taught her well.

And of course, Dugan being their mother's second
rite, the duchess jumped right on board with them. She
ed, praising Grizela for her brilliant idea. Clare's father,
o'd been discussing something with Wexford, turned his
ntion to what was going on around the table.

Clare was having none of it. This was the one time she
Wexford would be here to celebrate one of life's mile-
nes. She didn't want to share, not with her cousin, not
th anyone.

"No, absolutely not!" Clare exclaimed. "This ball is to
roduce Wexford to our friends and family. To celebrate
r marriage, not your upcoming nuptials."

"But Grizela has a good point, my dear," the duchess
id. "Everyone will be here anyway. Why not share the
oment?"

Clare threw her mother a hard look. "I should have
own you'd side with them. You can't allow me any happi-
ss. Not in your presence."

"Well, whatever you've done to win him over, I'm happy."
She smiled and finished off her whiskey.

"Your father is quite fascinating."

"He is." She put her glass down on a table beside her. "I
think I'm going to take a bath before dinner."

"The tub ought to be filling as we speak. I figured you'd
want to bathe before dressing for the evening."

Clare kissed him again. "You're so thoughtful. It's a pity
we don't have more time."

"I'm sure we could arrange something."

She shook her head. "No, my mother would come
looking for us herself if we were late. Now if it were Dugan,
that would be different."

He gathered her in his arms. "Come, let's not discuss
your cousin or anything else but us."

"Hmmm, that sounds wonderful," she replied. "I've been
meaning to ask, will we go straight to your country estate
near Stafford, or will we go to London?"

"I really need to check on things at the castle. Then we'll
go to London. Why?"

"No reason, I was just wondering."

Wexford began taking out her hair pins, one at a time. "I
have business at each."

"I will be glad to stay in one place for a while. It seems
like we've been traveling nonstop, from Brighton to Scotland
and then to Wexford Castle and on to Wexford House."

"I promise you, once I'm finished with my business, we'll
leave London and stay at the castle."

Clothes began to drop in a trail as she walked to the
bathing chamber. Wexford smiled and followed. She
climbed into the tub. "So what else did you and Papa talk
about? Horses?"

He nodded, the corners of his mouth curving up.

"Horses, estate management. He asked me what sort of business I was involved in. When I mentioned the canal, he was very interested."

"Papa would be someone reliable to talk to," she said. She slid farther into the tub. "Would you mind passing me that cake of soap?"

He passed her the soap and stood back, removing his clothes, one by one and placing them on the nearby chair. Clare gave him a sultry smile and made room for him in the tub.

16

Clare did her best to suffer through di[nner]. probably wouldn't haven't been as pol[ite] was if it were not for Wexford.

Her cousin, Dugan, and his betrothed had [come to] dinner. Dugan was as obnoxious as ever, his bet[rothed] w[as a] silly little slip of a girl who laughed and giggled a[t every]thing Dugan said when her cousin directed the conv[ersation] to her. Clare could tell by the way he acted things [would] change drastically once they married. She would be t[here to] give him an heir and perhaps a spare while he went [about] his business. She would be forced to look the other [way at] her husband's mistresses.

Dugan had been raised by Clare's parents aft[er the] untimely death of his own parents when he was te[n. He'd] been treated as a second son, and until he'd grown fr[om the] precious boy he'd been when he arrived, Clare ha[d] nothing but warm thoughts for him.

They were between courses. Grizela and Duga[n were] giggling and whispering about something. Why her [cousin]

"Oh, come now, Clare. Stop being so theatrical," Dugan said.

She stared at her cousin. "Theatrical? You want theatrical? Fine, you and your little tart can bask in all the well wishes, because I refuse to be part of such a charade."

Grizela had a smug look on her face, and Clare longed to wipe it right off, but she'd made her feelings known. She and Wexford wouldn't participate in such a travesty. She threw her napkin down on the table, stood, and, without further word, stormed out of the dining room.

Moments later, she slammed the door to the bedchamber, startling her lady's maid. She walked over to the windows and looked out. There was only a sliver of a moon, making it hard to see much of anything. She didn't care.

Wexford followed moments later. She didn't move her gaze from the faint moonlight dancing off the treetops.

"Are you all right?"

"It doesn't matter. I'm tired, Parr. I hadn't realized how tiring all this was until we arrived." She turned to face him. "Would it be terribly rude of us to simply leave and return to England? Then Grizela and Dugan can be the center of attention at Mother's ball, just as they wish."

"Do you think that wise? What of your father?"

"He'll go along with whatever I decide. He's the one person who actually understands."

"Then if leaving and going back to England is what will make you happy, we'll leave as soon as you're ready."

"Let's leave tomorrow. I don't want any of them trying to change my mind."

He wrapped his arms around her, drawing her close. "You're sure?"

"Yes."

"Then tomorrow it is. I'll inform your father this evening of our change of plans."

"Thank you."

He leaned down and kissed her soft lips. "Don't thank me yet, as I will demand repayment, my countess."

"Well, whatever you've done to win him over, I'm happy." She smiled and finished off her whiskey.

"Your father is quite fascinating."

"He is." She put her glass down on a table beside her. "I think I'm going to take a bath before dinner."

"The tub ought to be filling as we speak. I figured you'd want to bathe before dressing for the evening."

Clare kissed him again. "You're so thoughtful. It's a pity we don't have more time."

"I'm sure we could arrange something."

She shook her head. "No, my mother would come looking for us herself if we were late. Now if it were Dugan, that would be different."

He gathered her in his arms. "Come, let's not discuss your cousin or anything else but us."

"Hmmm, that sounds wonderful," she replied. "I've been meaning to ask, will we go straight to your country estate near Stafford, or will we go to London?"

"I really need to check on things at the castle. Then we'll go to London. Why?"

"No reason, I was just wondering."

Wexford began taking out her hair pins, one at a time. "I have business at each."

"I will be glad to stay in one place for a while. It seems like we've been traveling nonstop, from Brighton to Scotland and then to Wexford Castle and on to Wexford House."

"I promise you, once I'm finished with my business, we'll leave London and stay at the castle."

Clothes began to drop in a trail as she walked to the bathing chamber. Wexford smiled and followed. She climbed into the tub. "So what else did you and Papa talk about? Horses?"

He nodded, the corners of his mouth curving up.

"Horses, estate management. He asked me what sort of businesses I was involved in. When I mentioned the canal, he was very interested."

"Papa would be someone reliable to talk to," she said. She slid farther into the tub. "Would you mind passing me that cake of soap?"

He passed her the soap and stood back, removing his clothes, one by one and placing them on the nearby chair. Clare gave him a sultry smile and made room for him in the tub.

Clare did her best to suffer through dinner, and probably wouldn't haven't been as polite as she was if it were not for Wexford.

Her cousin, Dugan, and his betrothed had come for dinner. Dugan was as obnoxious as ever, his betrothed a silly little slip of a girl who laughed and giggled at everything Dugan said when her cousin directed the conversation to her. Clare could tell by the way he acted things wou change drastically once they married. She would be th give him an heir and perhaps a spare while he went a his business. She would be forced to look the other way her husband's mistresses.

Dugan had been raised by Clare's parents after the untimely death of his own parents when he was ten. He'd been treated as a second son, and until he'd grown from the precious boy he'd been when he arrived, Clare had had nothing but warm thoughts for him.

They were between courses. Grizela and Dugan were giggling and whispering about something. Why her mother had allowed them to sit directly alongside each other was beyond her when she and Wexford were placed across from one another.

"Grizela has a wonderful idea," Dugan announced. "Since you're having a ball for Clare and Wexford, Grizela suggested we announce our upcoming nuptials then. We'll do it again, of course, at her father and mother's ball, but since everyone will be here, why not?"

Why not indeed. Clare was seething at the very thought. This was her and Wexford's one time to celebrate the happiest event in their lives. Now, that scheming little tart had already figured out how to turn it around and make it about her and Dugan.

Her cousin had taught her well.

And of course, Dugan being their mother's second favorite, the duchess jumped right on board with them. She agreed, praising Grizela for her brilliant idea. Clare's father, who'd been discussing something with Wexford, turned his attention to what was going on around the table.

Clare was having none of it. This was the one time she and Wexford would be here to celebrate one of life's milestones. She didn't want to share, not with her cousin, not with anyone.

"No, absolutely not!" Clare exclaimed. "This ball is to introduce Wexford to our friends and family. To celebrate our marriage, not your upcoming nuptials."

"But Grizela has a good point, my dear," the duchess said. "Everyone will be here anyway. Why not share the moment?"

Clare threw her mother a hard look. "I should have known you'd side with them. You can't allow me any happiness. Not in your presence."

"Then tomorrow it is. I'll inform your father this evening of our change of plans."

"Thank you."

He leaned down and kissed her soft lips. "Don't thank me yet, as I will demand repayment, my countess."

"Oh, come now, Clare. Stop being so theatrical," Dugan said.

She stared at her cousin. "Theatrical? You want theatrical? Fine, you and your little tart can bask in all the well wishes, because I refuse to be part of such a charade."

Grizela had a smug look on her face, and Clare longed to wipe it right off, but she'd made her feelings known. She and Wexford wouldn't participate in such a travesty. She threw her napkin down on the table, stood, and, without further word, stormed out of the dining room.

Moments later, she slammed the door to the bedchamber, startling her lady's maid. She walked over to the windows and looked out. There was only a sliver of a moon, making it hard to see much of anything. She didn't care.

Wexford followed moments later. She didn't move her gaze from the faint moonlight dancing off the treetops.

"Are you all right?"

"It doesn't matter. I'm tired, Parr. I hadn't realized how tiring all this was until we arrived." She turned to face him. "Would it be terribly rude of us to simply leave and return to England? Then Grizela and Dugan can be the center of attention at Mother's ball, just as they wish."

"Do you think that wise? What of your father?"

"He'll go along with whatever I decide. He's the one person who actually understands."

"Then if leaving and going back to England is what will make you happy, we'll leave as soon as you're ready."

"Let's leave tomorrow. I don't want any of them trying to change my mind."

He wrapped his arms around her, drawing her close. "You're sure?"

"Yes."

17

Clare looked out the window as the carriage swayed over a rut in the road. It was the third day, and they were now back in northern England. The drystone walls and hedges rolled away in the distance among the green hills. Across from her, Parr dozed, his legs spread out. His eyes were shut. The daylight was fading.

Parr, having been jolted awake by the carriage hitting a pothole in the road, said quietly, "The road was washed out, so the coachman's taken us off the main road. We should come across an inn before long."

"Can't we turn around?"

"As I said, the main road has been washed out. We'll find an inn, unless, of course, you'd rather sleep on the side of the road," Parr said with a smile.

"Point taken," she replied with a sigh.

They rode along in silence.

"How much longer? Surely there's a village somewhere on this miserable road," she said finally. She was getting agitated by the delays and having to go out of the way.

A couple of hours later, her prayers were answered. They arrived at a remote inn, where Parr acquired them a room. At this late hour, the inn was nearly full, and Clare knew better than to complain upon finding herself in a small, simply furnished room.

The flames danced as she approached the little fireplace. Wexford had paid the innkeeper extra for more coal, along with having dinner served in their room. Roast mutton with potatoes, along with cheese and bread had been a welcome sight. Clare hadn't realized how hungry she was until she took a bite. Mutton was not one of her favorites, but tonight, it could have been a beef roast.

After dinner, Wexford excused himself. He was going to partake in some ale and see if he could get an idea of which way they needed to continue to get them back on the road to his country estate.

Clare drew back the bedclothes on the sturdy inn bed. The sheets appeared clean. She watched the firelight flicker on the walls until her eyes became heavy. Her thoughts drifted to her husband's. How many days would they have left to travel? Her thoughts became scattered, and she began to fall asleep.

She awoke sometime later, conscious someone was in bed with her. "Parr?"

He quieted her. "Don't speak," he whispered.

His mouth opened as he kissed her deeply, his tongue tangling with hers. She moaned as she felt him lift her chemise and pull it from her body. His hands began to explore, tenderly stroking her breasts before pinching her nipples.

"Parr," she moaned as she ran her palms over his nude back. His skin was hot as his muscles shifted under her hands and he settled his weight between her spread thighs.

"I'm here, my dove," he whispered as he nudged until he found her entrance and thrust inside.

He shifted back and rocked slowly, each thrust stretching her, pushing him in deeper. She arched up. He was in control, and he would have her in the manner he desired. He groaned and worked his hips a little faster, his cock all the way inside her. She felt each thrust as she received him over and over again.

His fingers slid down her side, between both their bodies, as he searched and finally found her moist feminine part. He pressed his thumb against her clitoris.

"Come, my dove," he whispered.

Slowly, she opened he eyes. Strands of his hair clung to his face, and his eyes stared into hers. His thumb circled her as his cock filled her. The pleasure was building, and he was in control.

She cried out his name as she went over the edge. He caught her shouts of pleasure with his mouth as he held her down with his hips as she came. She opened her eyes, gasping at the most intense pleasure she'd ever experienced.

He threw back his head, his eyes mad with lust. "My God," he ground out as his body jerked into hers and his seed flooded her. His head tilted back, his arms straight, but she couldn't see his face because of his damp hair. It was the most exquisite and life-altering moment of her existence.

"I love you," she whispered.

"And I love you, my heart. Always and forever."

He pulled out of her, lay on his side, and drew her close to him. His breath slowed and steadied as he slept.

He peered at Clare over his teacup the following morning. The breakfast the innkeeper's wife had provided was a rather tasty dish of eggs and freshly baked bread. She slathered jam on a piece of bread.

"We should reach Wexford Castle by tomorrow evening," he said.

"Really?"

He nodded and buttered another piece of warm bread. "If it looks as if we won't be able to make it sooner, I'm hoping we can go as far as my aunt's. She has a farm just to the north."

"That sounds interesting. I hope she won't be put off by unexpected guests."

"No, not at all. She'll be happy to see us since I haven't visited her in about two years."

She stood. "Excellent. I'm going to have the innkeeper's wife prepare us a luncheon in case we're not near an inn at that time."

"Excellent idea."

A half hour later, the horses were hitched and ready. Her husband joined her in the coach and knocked on the roof. Fog was rolling across the hills, which would make for an interesting journey. Then the carriage lurched forward.

He slumped in his seat as the hills went by. "Are you sorry we left your parents' home the way we did?"

"Absolutely not. Dugan and Charles have always been Mother's favorites, and I won't tolerate it anymore."

"Well, we will have to return, I suppose, for the wedding."

She rolled her eyes at him. "I can hardly wait."

"I hate that for you, that you feel that way."

She shook her head. "Don't be sorry for me. It's always been like this. Besides, you're my family now."

"You're right, and once we've returned, we'll have to bring all my siblings home for a private celebration."

She reached across and touched his hand. "Yes, we must. I know you miss them terribly."

"You have a soft heart, my love."

"Perhaps. I believe we should try to have more interaction with all of them."

"Alexandria does her best to help out."

"I know, but she also has her own life. Besides, you are the earl and now responsible for all of them."

"I'm aware of that. I tell you what, when we reach home, why don't you write my sister and find out where exactly each of them are. We'll invite everyone back home."

She smiled. "You mean to tell me you don't know where your siblings are?"

"Of course I do. The boys are at school, and my sisters? I believe they're staying with my aunt."

"Which aunt?"

"Aunt Hermione. She lives in London, is widowed, and immediately expressed an interest in helping out with my sisters."

"Getting them ready for their debut seasons?"

"Yes, among other things. They need to be ready to enter society."

"They also need to know that their brother loves them and is doing what's best for them. Don't leave them thinking they're not important to you."

"I can assure you, my dove, they know I love and care for each one of them."

Later that afternoon, they pulled up in front of Wexford's aunt's home. Clare barely had time to step from the carriage before Lady Thames was welcoming them. She was a stout, small lady whose rosy cheeks dimpled as she smiled at them.

"This is my bride, Auntie."

"Very happy to meet you. Please, do call me Aunt Gertrude."

Clare nodded.

Lady Thames led them inside. The interior had recently been redecorated. It was a lovely house with classic lines on the outside, and inside, a pink-and-white marble floor.

"Come," she said as she bustled down the hall. "The Marquess of Thames has been looking forward to meeting you."

Clare leaned over and whispered, "I thought you said she was widowed."

"I never said such a thing. Uncle Thomas is quite old, and, if I remember correctly, rarely leaves the house."

Lady Thames led them into a dark green sitting room. A tall man sat on a settee near the fire. His shock of white hair gave one a start. He stood, however, and bowed to Wexford.

"You must tell us all about your wedding. Alexandria wrote and said you'd eloped to Gretna Green."

"We did," he replied.

"There's a story, I'm sure," Aunt Gertrude said, her eyes dancing with mirth. "We wish you a long and very happy marriage, then,"

"Thank you, Auntie. That means the world to both of us."

Lady Thames turned to Clare. "I understand you're the daughter of the Duke of Renfrew."

"Yes, he's my father."

"Lord Thames met him once." She turned to her husband. "Didn't you, dear?"

"Yes, indeed, I had the privilege of meeting him a few years back."

Lady Thames seemed impatient with her husband's low manner. "I'm sure Lord Thames will love to share that story with you. In the meantime, I'm sure you'd both like to settle in after a day's worth of travel. I'll show you to your rooms," she said. "Dinner will be at eight sharp."

"Thank you, Auntie. That would be most appreciated," Wexford replied.

They followed the older woman through the entry hall and up the stairs. Wexford smiled as they began to ascend.

"I have fond memories of coming to spend summers here," Wexford said.

"As have I," his aunt replied, smiling. "Parr's parents traveled a great deal during the summer. His mother, the countess, didn't like leaving the children in only the governess's or nannies' care. We've never been able to have children of our own, so it was always a delight when they came."

Clare nodded as she imagined her husband and all his siblings running wild through the house without a care in the world. "I imagine he was a mischief maker."

"Oh, he was indeed," she replied with a hearty laugh.

Finally, they came to a pair of oak doors. A footman, who waited outside, threw open one door and they all entered. Inside was a large bedchamber in plum and lavender. In one corner near the window stood a small writing desk. The massive mahogany bed commanded attention from the wall it occupied. There was a fireplace with two gold chairs in front.

"This is beautiful, my lady."

"Thank you," she replied. Her gaze followed Wexford as he roamed the room. "Well, I'll let you two settle in. I'll see you at dinner."

With that, she disappeared from the room, leaving Clare and Wexford alone. Alone except for the sound of Agnes, Clare's maid, and Fitz, Wexford's valet, scurrying around in the dressing room adjacent to the main bedchamber.

"There is one person I want to stop and see on the way back. I need to talk to Angelo about this new canal, and I promise I won't take long," Wexford murmured as they got back on the road the following morning.

Clare found her husband's aunt and uncle to be fascinating and entertaining hosts. She looked forward to making a return visit or inviting the couple down to Wexford castle for a stay. She would discuss it with her husband once they returned, and perhaps have the younger children home when they did invite them.

Of course, it would all depend on what the midwife had to say.

"Angelo? I don't recall you mentioning anyone named Angelo."

"I may not have, my love. Angelo sees that my business ventures get where they need to be delivered along the canals. I wish to discuss the idea of building another canal with him."

"And he's along the way?"

"Yes."

"Then by all means, let us visit him."

They sat back, and Wexford pulled out a book he'd been reading during their travels. Clare did the same, and they both settled in.

After about two hours, Clare noted the sky darkening. It appeared as though rain would shortly be upon them, and she hoped they would be home or quite close to it before it did begin.

"It appears we're in for bad weather," Wexford said, putting down his book. "Let me tell the coachman to continue on rather than go to see Angelo today." He tapped on the roof of the coach to let the coachman know he wished to stop.

"But if it's important to you, we should go."

He shook his head. "No, I can see him another time. The rain will wash the roads out. We're almost home, and I'd rather get you there safe and sound than chance it, my love."

The coach stopped, and Wexford opened the door and jumped out. Clare could hear the two men, along with his valet, talking in muffled tones. She was thankful that he cared that much about her well-being, not wanting to be out on the roads when the rain did set in. If the clouds were any indication of what was to come, it was going to be wicked.

He quickly returned, and the carriage was on its way.

"How much farther?" she asked. None of the countryside, with its rolling hills, was familiar to her.

"About an hour," he replied, picking up his book once again. Clare wondered if he really was reading or if he were merely trying to lull himself into a more relaxed state. He worried her because he was always wound up as tight as a clock. He had an abundance of energy that few men she knew possessed.

Even at night, he slept few hours, more, however, after they made love. Even then, if he fell asleep, he would wake and leave their bed, unable to sleep anymore. She wondered what he did with his time. She hadn't heard any of the servants say, if they even knew. Perhaps he went to his study and took care of paperwork, or else she thought he might go to the library or sitting room and sit by a fire and read until sleep overtook him once more.

The motion of the carriage, combined with her thoughts, caused her to lull herself to sleep. It was a deep, peaceful sleep, in spite of them being in a rocking carriage. What awakened her was the cessation of all motion. The carriage was still, meaning they were home.

Hearing Wexford call out to her, Clare slowly opened her eyes. She glanced around until her vision homed in on the grand structure, a castle looming outside the carriage.

"We're home," he whispered.

A footman opened the door and set the steps. Wexford, not wanting anyone else to help his wife, quickly descended the steps and offered his hand to her. She put her hand on top of his and briefly smiled at him. When she came out of the carriage, the sky above was even darker than it had been.

Then the skies opened up and it began to rain, hard and fast as it plummeted toward the earth. Quickly, Wexford pulled her forward and into the dry and safe interior of the castle. She was home. They were home.

Inside the entrance hall, they were greeted by the sounds of Wexford's brothers and sister, which was unexpected as when he and Clare had left to go north, his siblings had been either in their respective schools or, in his sister's case, with Alexandria or Violet's good friend

Margaret Green, daughter of the Duke of Somerset. With those two, where one went, the other followed.

They all clamored around him. "Parr, Parr, where have you been?"

Wexford put his hand up to silence everyone. "First of all, what are you all doing here? I wasn't expecting you."

Violet, being the oldest, spoke for them. "Alexandria sent us here. She said something about you going to Scotland, but that you would return shortly."

"But the boys? Weren't you both in school, or did you two get into some mischief making?"

George and Gregory, identical twins and the youngest, said nothing, but looked as though they were trying to wish themselves as far away as they could go.

"We'll discuss it later," Wexford replied. He took Clare's hand. "There's someone I'd like for you all to meet, and for that, I'm glad we're all together."

"Except for Alexandria. She's not here," young Jenny spoke up.

"You're right," Wexford said. He continued, his hand still holding Clare's smaller one. "I would like to introduce you all to Clare, my wife."

Clare smiled at each of them. "It's so nice to finally meet all of you. Parr has told me so much about each and every one of you."

They were still standing in the hall, which had a damp feeling to it, with the rain pouring outside.

"Come," Wexford said. "Let's go to the blue room where it's warmer by far. Then you can each introduce yourselves to Clare."

Feet scurried and giggles were heard as the four Parr siblings scampered quickly into a room done in the most exquisite shade of blue Clare thought she'd ever seen. She could only describe it as a China blue, like the porcelain pieces that came from that area of the world.

Clare sat on a dark blue settee as each of her husband's brothers and sisters came forward and introduced themselves.

"I'm Violet, and I'm the oldest of us four," Violet said demurely. Unlike her siblings, she had sable-brown hair and dark chocolate-brown eyes. A striking contrast to her blond-haired, blue-eyed brothers and sisters.

"It's very nice to finally meet you, Violet."

George stepped forward and introduced himself, followed by Gregory. It was hard for Clare to distinguish which one was which, but Parr whispered to her that she'd very quickly learn.

Jenny came forward next. She was the shiest one, as her husband had told her. "I'm Jennifer, but everyone calls me Jenny."

"It's very nice to meet you, Jenny."

For the next hour, Clare and Parr listened to all of them tell their stories of what they had been doing while waiting for them to return to the castle. Finally, seeing the boys were restless and the girls looking like they would flee if given the chance, Wexford excused them all.

Clare called for tea after the door shut behind them.

Wexford paced the room. "I need to write Alexandria and find out what's going on."

"Why don't you speak with the boys before you do? Find out what's going on with them. It might be nothing. Hear it from them before writing your sister. The girls too."

He sat in a chair next to the settee upon which she was seated. "You're right, and thank you for welcoming them so warmly."

"We're all family now, Parr. They've been through a lot in

their young lifetimes. Losing your parents... It's hard no matter what your age."

A knock came on the door, and the tall, gray-headed, aging butler appeared with tea. He set the tray down on the table in front of Clare.

"Thank you, Finch," Wexford said.

Finch nodded and pulled a letter out of an inside pocket of his coat. "This came for you. I was told to give it only to you, and not to make mention of it to any of the other children."

He passed it to Wexford, who took it and studied the writing on it. "Thank you, Finch. That'll be all for now."

The older man nodded once again and quit the room as quietly as he'd appeared. Wexford waited until the door closed before he broke the seal on the letter.

"It's from Alexandria," he told Clare.

"Hopefully, it'll contain answers to your questions," she replied. Clare began to prepare tea for them both, adding the cream and sugar to her husband's and just cream to her own before pouring the tea over it. She passed it to Wexford, who still sat, letter in hand as though trying to decide whether or not he should read it.

He accepted the cup with one hand, setting it down on the table to cool, then he opened the missive. He scanned the contents before adjusting himself in the chair. He read the letter in detail, the room eerily quiet except for the sound of a clock ticking in the corner.

Wexford said nothing, and when he finished rereading the letter, he folded it and put it in his coat pocket. He then picked up his teacup and took a long, thoughtful sip.

"Well, are you going to keep me in suspense forever?" Clare asked.

His face was solemn. "The boys have been sent home for

the summer. Evidently, they were making mischief. They can return in the autumn."

"Boys will be boys," Clare replied.

"Yes, well, it's not the boys who concern me. It's Violet."

Clare put down her teacup. "What about her?"

"Alexandria says she's been ruined, and the real problem is that the man involved is married."

"What? Are they sure?"

Wexford nodded and sighed. "Yes, I'm afraid so. Alexandria was the one who caught them."

"I don't have to tell you what this does to her."

"Yes, I'm well aware of the consequences, and now we know why Alexandria wanted her out of London."

"Don't confront her with it for a day or two, Parr. I'm sure she's scared to death knowing that you know. It'll give you both time to think."

"You're right, and I'll wait to talk to her. If I did right now, I'm sure I wouldn't handle it well."

She reached over to him. He took her hand in his and squeezed. "I could speak with her. She might open up more readily to me. You know, me being a woman and all, and not a scary older brother. Just let me know what you want me to do."

"I don't wish to involve you in these matters. She's my sister. I ought to be able to talk with her as we always have."

She squeezed his hand tightly and looked squarely into his eyes. "We're all family now. This is also a delicate matter, and she may feel embarrassed having to speak with you about it."

He sat there for a moment, his square jawline twitching as he contemplated his options. "You're right. You are part of this family now, and I'm sure you'll be able to speak more freely with my younger sisters than I am able to do."

"It's a sensitive subject matter for all involved."

"You are right. Talk to her, see if she'll confide in you. I'll wait to approach her about it for a day or two. But no longer, and you shall tell me everything that happened."

Clare nodded. "Of course I will. Unless, of course, it's something she tells me in confidence, then I'm afraid I can't."

Wexford gave her a lopsided grin. "If you were a man, I could see you as a politician."

"Really? That still doesn't change the fact that I won't betray her confidence unless, and only unless, it's life-threatening."

"Very well, but you must let her know she and I are going to have the conversation at some point."

She smiled demurely at her husband. "Yes, one of the many I'm sure you're going to have with all of them."

"You're included in that too, madam."

"Oh, I'm sure I am," she teased.

19

Wexford rose early as usual. He always liked to start his day with a brisk ride. Today was no different. When he'd left Clare in their bed, she was sound asleep, a contented smile on her lips. Such a temptation, but one he had to pass on. After his ride, he would have breakfast before going to his study. There was much to be done, ledgers to catch up on, and now, with all his younger siblings in the house, their needs to be seen to.

Taking the reins of Hercules, he mounted and headed out across a field. He wanted to ride to the brook that ran into a small river which formed the boundary on the south side of the property. It flowed down to the nearby village from there.

Wexford had always loved coming to this exact location as a boy. The sound of the babbling brook relaxed him. He'd spent hours here hiding from his father and the endless responsibilities his father imposed on him. He was his father's heir and as such was still schooled even when not at school. Schooling at the family's ancestral seat meant learning of a different kind. Here he'd been educated about the estate, the land, how to read it. What sort of crops were grown and when. What animals were raised, and for what. He was taught how to read ledgers, what was paid, when, and why.

There had been very little time left for boyish endeavors such as swimming in the brook. No, his father's expectations were far higher than those of what a normal boyhood brought. The earl had mapped out his life. There was no time for Parr to be a mere boy.

Still, he'd never forgotten this spot. He still came here whenever he needed solitude. Someday, he would bring his own son or sons and teach them to fish. He would do many things his father never had.

Unfortunately, his younger siblings were all in residence, and it was time he rode back to the house for breakfast. Perhaps later, in the afternoon, he could ride with George and Gregory. He had no intention of being like their father and ignoring them when they were home from school. He knew better than any of them the importance of family, or the lack of it.

It wasn't that his father hadn't been a good father. He merely was of the age, as was his mother, that believed children were to be schooled and their lives formed by nannies and governesses. It was Parr's job to see to it the boys had some fun in their otherwise mundane lives.

He would spend time with his two sisters, Jenny and Violet, but he would leave the curious side of the feminine sex to Clare. She seemed to have won them over, and who better than she?

Wexford headed his horse back in the direction of the house. He urged the stallion into a gallop, letting the beast stretch his legs and run out any pent-up restlessness the beast had. Finding suitable horses for each of his siblings was something he would discuss with the stable master. None of them had ever had their own mounts, just whatever was deemed suitable for their present stage of riding.

After handing Hercules over to a groom, he found Clare seated in the breakfast room alone. She wore a light blue muslin dress which was high waisted in the fashion of the day. She was finishing off a plate of eggs and toast.

He bent down and kissed her on the cheek. "Good morning, my love. Where is everyone?"

"I understand it is customary for the children to take their meals in the nursery, so that is where they are. I did, however, tell Cook that would change beginning in the morning."

He sat down and waited until the footman finished placing a plate in front of him. "Good. I think it's important for everyone to spend time together. Our father saw to it that we took our meals upstairs. I plan to change that. We'll all take our meals together."

"I believe that's important as well. My father always had my brother and me having our meals with my mother and him," she replied. "Dinner always depended on what they had planned, if they had guests, or were going out."

He began to slather jam onto a piece of toast as they talked. "I need to spend a couple of hours in my study to go over the accounts. Then I thought I'd take Gregory and George riding. What have you planned?"

"I thought Violet, Jenny, and I could spend the morning together. I'd like to find out what each of them is interested in. I hope in the next day or two, the three of us could make a trip into the village. I'm sure a day of shopping would be welcome."

"I know it will be. What if we all went on a picnic tomorrow?"

"That would be wonderful."

"Good. I thought the boys and I could fish in the brook."

She nibbled on a piece of golden-brown toast. "May I ask you something?"

"But of course, my heart. What is it?"

"I know the boys are your heirs until we have a son of our own, but who is the elder of the two, Gregory or George?"

"Gregory. Gregory is older by about five minutes, or so I was always told. Why?"

"Just curious.

"Unfortunately, my father never really knew how they were to be schooled. I've decided they should be taught as though they both are the heir. At least for a while, then Gregory will be groomed."

"I think that's a very sound idea. They appear to be close, and it would be hard to imagine them being separated."

"Agreed, though it will happen at some point. I believe they already are in separate classes at school," Wexford replied, and winked at Clare. "At least we can do all this until we have a son of our own."

"Yes," she said.

They ate in silence for a few minutes. Wexford had begun to speak when the door opened and all four of his younger siblings came rushing in. He wondered what they were up to. The boys were always into some mischief, and the girls, well, his sisters might appear to be quiet and girlish, but deep down, they loved nothing better than to best one of their brothers at something.

This ought to be interesting. So far, Clare had been able to hold her own with them, but that might change the more at ease his brothers and sisters became with her. Growing up for her had been considerably different, with only her brother to worry about playing pranks on her.

ONE MOMENT, CLARE WAS ENJOYING A QUIET BREAKFAST WITH her husband, the next, they were overrun by four very excited young persons. They were inundated with questions by all parties. The group sounded like a flock of magpies, everyone speaking at once.

Finally, Parr took control of the group and their madness.

"Sit down!" he commanded.

All four did as they were asked, but immediately started up with their questions aimed at both her and her husband.

"One at a time, if you please!" he further demanded.

Everyone managed to stay quiet. Clare let her husband dictate how this would go.

"Violet, you are the oldest of you four. What is it you need to know?" he asked quietly.

"It isn't fair," Gregory said with some authority in his voice. "She and Jenny always get to go first."

"I'll get to you in a minute, Gregory," he replied and turned his attention on to Violet. "Go ahead, Violet."

"What are we going to do today?"

Clare responded, "I thought you, Jenny, and I could spend the morning together. We can go through all your wardrobe and see if there's anything either of you need. We'll make a list and go shopping in the village in a day or so."

"We need some embroidery threads," Jenny said quietly. "Might we be able to get some?"

"Of course. Add it to our list," Clare replied.

Gregory had his turn and was quite satisfied that he and his brother would be riding with their older brother that afternoon.

"You and I will visit with the tenants at some point. It'll do you good to meet them since you may one day be earl."

"May I come along?" George inquired.

Gregory glared at his brother. "No, you may not."

Wexford intervened on what was obviously a delicate topic. Gregory had long ago established himself as the heir and was not the sort to share. Not even when that person was his own brother and twin.

"You may come along, George. I'm glad to see you taking an interest, and it will do the tenants good to see you both."

"May we go to town as well?" George inquired.

"Write out what it is you need and present it to me in two hours," Wexford replied. He turned to Jenny. "Jenny, do you have a question?"

"Where will you send us when summer ends?"

Clare glanced at Wexford as he sat back in his chair to contemplate her question.

"Let's not worry about that for the present. I want you all to enjoy your summer. There'll be plenty of time to discuss these matters."

"Unless you're Gregory or me, you'd know you'd be returning to school," George crowed.

"It's different for your sisters, as both of you know," Clare offered.

"Girls are always treated special," Gregory said.

Clare tapped her fingers on the table, carefully thinking of how she should answer his statement, but Wexford beat her to it.

"As they should be."

Gregory's answer was to change the subject. He turned

to his brother. "If we're to ride with Parr this afternoon, we need better horses. Not the ponies we've always ridden."

"May we go see what the stablemaster has available, Parr?"

"Yes, of course," Wexford replied. "Before all of you go scurrying off, I want to share something with you. Rather than eat breakfast in the nursery, you may join us here. Same for the midday meal and dinner. I think you're all old enough to be treated as young adults."

They all stared at their older brother as though he'd grown two heads. Then, realizing he was quite serious, they cheered and let on with merriment. Clare was again unsure how to take it all in. They certainly were a different bunch of siblings.

After they filed out of the breakfast room, Clare poured a fresh cup of tea. "That went rather well, wouldn't you say?"

"It did, though I'm concerned about Gregory and his attitude."

"Has he always been like that?"

"No, it's something recent he's developed since I've become earl. He and George will be off to school in the autumn. I'm hoping he'll grow out of it."

Clare nodded. "What will they do after school?"

"I've thought to purchase a commission for one of them. Gregory most likely. George has a head for figures and an interest in estate management. I might find a way for him to utilize his skills either here or one of my other estates." He smiled and began to scrape his chair back in order to stand. "Luckily, it isn't something that must be decided today."

"No," she replied solemnly.

Wexford hesitated. "Is there something else, my dove? Something about the girls?"

"No, not right now. I need to set up a meeting with the

housekeeper to go over things with her, and see if there's anything needed."

"Very good. Then I'll leave you to my sisters and other household matters." He kissed her on the cheek before quitting the room. Clare watched longingly at his retreating figure.

She finished her cup of tea and beckoned one of the footmen. "Would you ask Mrs. Brown to bring another tea tray for two, and to join me in the drawing room?"

The young man looked startled, but did his best to cover it up. "Yes, my lady. I'll go tell her now."

"Thank you." She pushed her chair back, stood and headed to the drawing room, where she found a fire in the fireplace, taking any chill off the room. Walking to the French doors, Clare peered out at the garden. She hoped Jenny and Violet would give her enough time to meet with the housekeeper. There was much to be discussed. She wasn't sure if her husband had just let Mrs. Brown run the house as she saw fit, not giving a second glance to items purchased or if he was mindful of everything that went on in his house. Afterward, the girls would be a welcome diversion. She wanted to get to know both of them better. Jenny, given her young age, seemed a bit more high-strung than Violet. Clare had the feeling that Violet's façade was simply a brick wall so she didn't have to let those around her know the true Violet.

She was sitting on a couch in front of the fire when Mrs. Brown entered, making her thoughts of the girls evaporate. Mrs. Brown was a matronly woman, older and more mature. She'd been at the house for over twenty years.

"You wished to see me, my lady?" she asked, setting down a tray with a teapot and two cups on a nearby table.

"I thought you might join me in a cup of tea. That is if

you can take the time out of your busy schedule." Clare knew the woman probably kept a tight-running household and she'd taken her away from her well-ordered comfort zone.

Mrs. Brown seated herself in a nearby chair, her spine ramrod straight as she waited for Clare to finish preparing their tea.

"I thought we should get to know each other, that you could explain how you run the house, how things have been done all these years."

"Indeed I can, my lady. Would you like to see the books as well?"

"We'll do that another time. I know you've got your hands full, and as I said, I thought it would be wise if we got to know each other," she replied. "Also, perhaps you can give me your thoughts on each of the staff, particularly those under your charge."

Clare sat back and listened as Mrs. Brown named everyone and their function, and whether they were proficient at their position. She then explained in an abbreviated form how the house was run. Up until now, Wexford had pretty much let Mrs. Brown run the house as she saw fit. Clare quickly decided as she made notes that she didn't want to make any changes; at least not yet. The house was well cleaned, no dust on any surfaces she'd found so far. The sheets and towels were white and clean and neatly in their places. So, for now, she'd leave things.

"Would you care to go over the menu with Mrs. Wayfield, my lady?" the housekeeper asked as things between them were winding down.

"Set up a convenient time to meet with her. I'm to meet with Violet and Jenny, and I know they won't want to spend too much time tied to me. Tell her I'll stop by the kitchens when we're finished."

"Very well, my lady. Is there anything else?"

"No, that's all for now, and Mrs. Brown, you are doing an outstanding job running this house. I think you and I will get along quite well."

"Thank you, my lady. We were quite excited when we learned the earl had finally taken a wife. Please let me know if there's anything you need."

Clare waited until she heard the sound of the door closing behind Mrs. Brown before she poured herself another cup of tea. She knew the girls should be arriving any moment. Shopping was probably the first thing on their minds, which she intended to put off for a few days.

Her top priority was Violet and seeing if she could get her to talk about this dilemma she had gotten herself into. What hadn't Alexandria told them? There were so many different things that could be misconstrued for ruining a young lady. Depending on the situation, it might be something as simple as a lengthy kiss or being alone in the company of a young man longer than appropriate.

If Violet were truly ruined, if she'd been bedded, it would change things. If the man were married, that fact alone would change things drastically. What if there were a child? Even if there were not, she and Parr would need to figure out where to send Violet for at least a year. Word would spread throughout the ton either way, if it hadn't already. Violet would be the talk of every gossip in town. For now, until they knew for sure, Violet staying here would be the best solution.

She was wondering how she should even broach the topic with young girl when the drawing room door was flung open and Violet and Jenny appeared. They sat in respective chairs as they discussed plans for the summer. It was Violet herself who brought up her recent indiscretion.

"I'm sure Alexandria told you much, though if I were you, I wouldn't believe what our dear sister insinuated," Violet said with some authority.

"Why don't you tell me yourself? That way, we keep Alexandria out of it."

"I'm in agreement with that."

"So, are these rumors true—that you've been ruined?"

"Ruined is such a vulgar word," Violet replied. She tapped the arm of her chair with her finger as she pondered the rest of her answer. "A lady can be considered ruined by simply being alone with a man, no matter if it's the two of them in a room or if they're strolling in a garden out of sight of anyone else. Or it can mean when a man's compromised a woman's virtue. The choices are many."

Clare tried to maintain her composure. Parr had warned her that Violet could be overly dramatic, and she was certain that was what was occurring right now. "You still haven't answered the question. It's a simple one, I believe. Have you or have you not been ruined? And if so, in what manner?"

"Do you really think you and Parr can keep me from him?" Violet taunted, cheekily ignoring Clare's question.

"He's married, Violet, though I don't know who he is. You'll never be able to have him."

"Then what difference does it make?"

"None, I suppose, unless there's a child involved," Clare replied, picking up her cup of tea.

Violet sprang from her chair and stood before the fire. "What are you going to tell Parr?"

"That you've been most uncooperative. I will also recommend that perhaps an arranged marriage would be the best route for you, although that would involve a distasteful deception. I'm sure he can find someone, and if you're wed quickly, no one would ever question the timing of a babe's birth, if there indeed is one growing in your belly as we speak. Or we can send you to the country until...you are fit to rejoin society."

Violet turned pale, and then her cheeks grew red as the gravity of her situation must have taken root at last. In a subdued tone, she pleaded, "At least let me have some say in whom I marry. Host a ball with any available men. I'll make my choice."

"I'll mention it to Parr. I don't see where he'd object. Just know that you'll marry one of the men he invites."

There was silence as Clare finished her tea. Jenny fidgeted in her chair for a moment.

"Are we still going to go through our wardrobes and write up a list of things we need?" she asked.

Clare smiled at her. "Of course we are. Why don't I get a pencil and some paper and we'll go do that. By the time we finish, it'll be time for luncheon."

She walked over to the nearby desk and gathered her supplies. They started out together, and Violet, with the resilience of the young, seemed to return to her normal energetic self. The girls informed her what each needed, and then the room grew quiet as Clare made notes. When she looked up, the sisters had snuck out, headed upstairs to their rooms.

Clare shook her head. She was dreading the conversation she needed to have with her husband in regards to his sister. Violet still hadn't given her a clear answer. Maybe Wexford would have better luck.

20

"How can she not take the repercussions of her actions seriously?" Wexford asked, shaking his head as he stood before the fire with a brandy in hand. It was after dinner, and his brothers and sisters had excused themselves and left them alone.

Clare had told him of her conversation earlier in the day with Violet. At first, Wexford wanted to confront his sister and tell her what would happen next, but Clare had prevailed. She didn't want her husband speaking with his sister when he wasn't in control of his temper or emotions.

"Viscount Hale has shown an interest in her. Perhaps I should pursue it. I'll see how serious he is," Wexford said.

"He's quite a bit older, with three grown daughters of his own, isn't he?" Clare asked.

"Yes, but under the circumstances, Violet really doesn't have many options. Besides, Hale is wealthy, and I doubt he'd be in need of Violet's dowry."

"Why don't we give her the option? Hold a party, invite men whom you know are in search of a wife. If nothing transpires from that, you could then approach Hale."

Wexford shook his head. "Hale would know there'd been no other suitors if we waited."

"I don't think you're going to have to worry about Violet finding a young man. It just needs to be done quickly."

He could see this wasn't going to be an easy matter, and one that wouldn't be solved in one day. Giving in to Clare's suggestion was probably the best solution to an otherwise tedious situation. "Very well, plan your party. Just keep it small. I'll furnish you with a list of whom to invite and what single gentlemen need an invitation."

"That would be so much help. It can be held in two weeks?"

"If you can put it together, we'll host it."

He needed to sit down and give this some serious thought. With whom exactly would he like his sister matched up? Violet was headstrong, and he knew he had to keep her focused. Otherwise, she would take control and find a man who would be an undesirable match for her, and if he allowed a marriage to proceed, it would be disastrous.

"Let me think on possible suitors. I'll have a list of them and other guests in the morning."

"Thank you." She smiled at him as he swallowed his brandy.

"Did you get everything else you wanted accomplished done?"

"Yes, the girls wrote out a list of things they need. We also went through their wardrobes. They're going to require a few new things. We'll go into the village in a day or two to shop," she replied. "How about you? Did you have a good day with Gregory and George?"

"Yes, I think we did, and it's exactly what they both need, time away from their studies."

"They seem like they're good boys. They just need

someone like you to show them the way. It is an awkward time in their lives."

Wexford smiled and poured another brandy. "They are, and so are Violet and Jenny."

"Violet needs some guidance right now."

"I know, and I think she'll be all right. I'm just afraid she'll make an irrational decision."

"Which is why you're going to make out a list of possible suitors. The sooner we plan this party and put the names in front of her, the more likely it is she's going to want to choose one."

Wexford sat next to her on the couch she'd been occupying since dinner. He leaned over and kissed her. "You're doing splendidly with them. I can't wait for our own child to get here."

Instinctively, she placed a hand on her stomach. She had been quite intuitive from the moment she thought she was with child. She'd begun to make the babe little things for when it arrived, even if her sewing skills weren't as good as others'. This was her and Wexford's child, something conceived out of love. Their love.

She smiled at him and returned to the topic at hand. "Violet is quite opinionated and has quite the sharp tongue on her for someone so young. Has she always been like that?"

"Sadly, yes, but she reminds me a great deal of you when we first met," he replied. "Why do you ask?"

"I'm afraid that earlier, my attempt to clarify the manner of her ruination was rewarded with her mockery and defiance."

"She likes to shock people."

Clare sighed. "If I were any other lady, I'm sure she would have succeeded."

"What brings this up? Surely you don't doubt yourself, do you?"

She shook her head, but didn't look at him directly. "No, I don't doubt myself. Some of Violet's answers caught me unprepared, that's all. I suppose I'll grow into my role. By the time any daughters we might have are Violet's age, I'll be well versed in the ways of young women."

He took her hands in his and squeezed. "Clare, never doubt yourself about anything. You are the love of my heart and will be for the rest of my life. Nothing you can say or do will ever change that."

"But? I sense there's something more you aren't saying?"

"No, there is not. However, should you have a problem with any of my sisters or brothers that you are unable to handle, please come to me. Don't let it grow inside you. Remember, we're in this together."

Her eyes filled with tears. "Thank you for your support. I don't know what I did to get so lucky in finding you."

"We found each other. With some help from Clevedon, of course," he replied and kissed the back of her hand. "Are you ready to retire for the evening?"

"Yes."

After he helped her rise from the couch, she wandered closer to the fireplace, and he followed. He stood, his legs braced apart. One hand came up to cup her face. She closed her eyes as his mouth descended on hers. He parted his lips over hers and licked at the seam with his tongue, trying to coax a response.

She opened for him, and he pressed his tongue deep into her mouth, exploring her depths. She kissed him back, opening her mouth wider, angling her head just right, touching his tongue with her own.

Heat rose between them in a surge of passion. He

wrapped one hand about her waist, the other holding her close by the hips. He drew her firmly against him. She was then quite aware of his hard, muscled thighs, and of his masculinity. She needed his maleness close to her, craved every inch of his body. Her arms snaked about his neck as her body strained against his. She wanted to be closer.

He lifted his head and looked down at her. "Shall we retire, Lady Wexford?"

"Yes," she replied breathlessly.

Inside their bedchamber, he led her to the mattress and laid her down. He pulled off her shoes and stockings, then unlaced her dress before pulling it over her hips. Off came her dress, and anything else between them. Wexford sat on the side of the bed and took off his boots, then the rest of his clothes.

Then his weight was on her. His hands were beneath her, tilting her as he came inside her in one firm thrust. He braced some of his weight on his forearms and began moving, setting a firm and fast-paced rhythm.

Suddenly, everything shattered as though there had been an explosion deep inside. Rather than pain, it was an urge. An urge to have him close by. Wexford growled as he collapsed on her and the liquid heat of his body filled her, leaving them hot and slick with sweat.

The intimate act had been very pleasurable, making her eyes heavy, as well as his. Her eyes drifted closed, and she floated off to sleep.

They share their love one more time in the early hours of dawn. She awoke to warmth as he moved his hands between her thighs and found her hot and wet for him. He probed with the fingertips of one hand stroking her gently, parting her folds, sliding one finger up inside her, until he could wait no longer.

"You are ready," he whispered huskily.

"Yes."

He entered her in one thrust, his eyes closed. He stayed on his knees between her thighs, and watched her face as he withdrew and entered again and again. Wexford smelled the rawness of their sex as he concentrated on giving her his full length, and listened to the natural rhythm of what they were doing.

His rhythm steady, Wexford thrust into her tight wet passage. He entered her one more time, shuddering, pushing deep as his seed filled her.

She was almost asleep when he pulled the bedcovers up over their damp bodies. He slid one arm beneath her head before closing his eyes and began falling asleep. Just before he fell asleep, she turned over on her side and burrowed her head against his shoulder and sighed contently.

———

CLARE WAS SITTING IN THE BREAKFAST ROOM ALONE WHEN Parr walked in. She was wearing a rose-colored day dress, her hair swept up off her shoulders. She smiled at him as he moved to his chair.

"Good morning," he said. "I take it everyone has had breakfast and are now otherwise occupied?"

She nodded demurely. "Yes." She picked up a scone that had been sitting on her plate and took a bite.

"Are you taking them to the village today?"

"Yes, this afternoon. My one stipulation to them was they would help with the invitations to our soiree."

"Did you have the list of possible suitors you spoke of yesterday?"

"Besides Viscount Hale?"

"Yes."

"Who are they?"

He sat back in his chair as a footman placed a plate in front of him. "George Sutton, Viscount Alderbury, and Phillip Marker, Marquess of Ashwood. The marquess has always had a soft spot in his heart for Violet, and she seems fond of him."

"So we have three possible suitors. That will work well," she replied. "I'll come to your study after breakfast and get their information from you."

"Yes, but let's wait until the invitations have gone out to tell Violet."

"You know I never got an answer from her about how or if she really was compromised," Clare said.

"I'm looking into it."

"You aren't going to ask the gentleman involved directly, are you? He's married." Clare tried not to look horrified and instead picked up her cup of tea and pretended it needed refilling.

"Of course not. At least not now. If the time comes where I must, I will. I've a friend who knows the gentleman."

"I thought no one knew for sure who it was?" Clare asked.

"A name keeps coming up. Alderbury mentioned him to me."

Clare rolled her eyes in disgust. "I suppose you're not going to share this information with me?"

"When I have all my facts, I promise I will."

"Thank you. Now I suppose I should find the girls so we can get started."

He pulled a piece of paper off his desk. "Here, you might want this. It's the list of people I thought should be invited."

She scanned the names. "This will be nice. Nothing too big or pretentious."

He came nearer and kissed her. "This will be perfect."

"I certainly hope so. Is there anything you want from the village?"

"No, but enjoy yourself with my sisters. Don't let them buy the shops out."

Clare turned to leave, paper in hand. "I'll see you later this afternoon."

He smiled. "Yes, you will."

Clare headed upstairs to the girl's bedchambers. There was so much to be done, but one afternoon in the village wouldn't make much difference. It would give her time to get to know her two sisters-in-law and learn their likes and dislikes.

She found them in Violet's room. Jenny sat on the bed while Violet sat at her dressing table while her maid was fussing with her hair.

"I'll be ready to leave momentarily," Violet announced.

Clare tried not to let a smile cross her lips. "Don't forget, we're going to spend an hour doing invitations this morning. I've ordered the carriage brought around then."

"I can't! My fingers will be stained! What will people think?" Violet exclaimed.

"No one will see your fingers. You'll be wearing gloves, silly," Jenny said as she sat up on the bed where she'd be lounging across the mattress.

"Jenny's right. Besides it's only for an hour." Clare turned to leave. "I decided to have everything set up in the dining room. I'll see you momentarily."

"It's not fair that I have to do such menial things," Violet wailed.

"I only asked you to help with the invitations, Violet.

With three of us, we should be able to get the majority of them written and addressed."

"Very well, but I expect some say in the available young men being invited," Violet retorted.

Clare, who'd been looking at a painting of a field of tulips on the wall, spun around and faced her young sister-in-law. "Why? Is there someone in particular you'd like invited?" She knew she had to maintain her composure as Violet loved to shock people. "I know Parr has Viscount Hale on his list along with Viscount Alderbury and the Marquess of Ashwood."

"Ugh, he needn't bother inviting Viscount Hale. He's old. The other two will do, but that's all? Three?"

"Viscount Hale has expressed an interest in courting you, which is why Parr is inviting him," Clare replied. "We'll go over the list as we write out the invitations. If there's someone you'd like invited, we can discuss it with Wexford."

"Very well, but I will decline any advances from Hale. The man is too old."

Jenny, who had been quiet all this time listening to the conversation, stood and gazed at her sister. "Hale might be old, but he's very wealthy."

Violet dismissed her maid and stood. "Shall we? The sooner we spend an hour writing is an hour closer to going to the village."

Violet led the group out of her bedchamber and down to the dining room, where three places were set up with parchment and pens. She grabbed the list and began scanning the names on it.

"What about the Earl of Bath? I don't see his name on the list."

Clare arched a brow at her sister-in-law as she scrutinized her. "Parr mentioned the earl and countess have gone to the continent for the summer. Why, do you know the countess well?"

"Er, no, but I know Parr is friends with the earl."

Clare said nothing further. She couldn't recall hearing the earl's name other than in passing, so she doubted they were such good friends as Violet was trying to have her believe. Could the Earl of Bath be the mysterious man who had supposedly ruined Violet?

"This isn't a long list, Clare," Jenny said after they'd begun writing.

"Parr and I thought it would be best to keep it smaller since a lot of people he would like to invite are on holiday or at their country estates."

"That is indeed wise," Jenny replied.

"It's our first social event as a married couple, so smaller is better."

Violet rolled her eyes, something she seemed to be particularly fond of doing. "Plus you're trying to get me married off as quickly and quietly as possible."

Jenny shook her head. "Don't pay her any mind. Violet always thinks everything is about her."

Clare tried to concentrate on the invitation she was writing out, knowing she best not smile and let Violet catch her doing it.

They continued on in silence for a few minutes more. Clare heard Violet sigh, a way to let everyone know she was bored and ready to move on to something else. They'd been at it for around an hour and were about finished. Clare finished her invitation, addressed it, sealed it, and put it to the side.

"Finish what you're doing. I think it's time to go into the village. I'm going to go gather my things. I'll meet you both by the front door."

The girls squealed and put their heads down to complete their tasks. Clare smiled as she left the room. Wexford would certainly be curious about his sister's interest in the Earl of Bath. It was obvious that without being pushed, Violet had all but told her the earl was most likely her lover, or whatever he really was to Violet.

21

Guests began to arrive two days before the soiree was to start. The guest rooms had been aired out and thoroughly cleaned, as was the entire house. An air of excitement had settled in among staff and family alike.

Not all the guests were staying with them, just a few who'd come a long way. Several others had family nearby or were staying at the local inn.

Clare had made room for the three bachelor guests since none of them deemed it necessary to take a room at the village inn. They were friends of her husband's and obviously had matters to catch up on. She put them in one wing, far away from the stairs leading to Violet's and Jenny's rooms and away from the other guests.

Wexford planned hunting, skeet shooting, and riding as outdoor activities to keep the gentlemen occupied during the day. Billiards, cards, and whatever activities Clare had thought to arrange would take up the evenings.

George and Gregory were ecstatic to learn Parr was including them in most of the outdoor activities. Gregory in particular felt this meant he was quite grown up and above being treated as a child, whereas George understood his place. George knew he and his brother were in that in between place where they were no longer children, but they were not adults either.

Clare was thankful she had such an efficient staff to handle all the details of readying the house for the guests. To make things even better, the weather seemed to be cooperating. The days were warm and pleasant and the evenings the same until late at night. The superb weather also meant she could serve some meals out on the terrace overlooking the gardens. The guests seemed to appreciate the change.

Which was why on the day before the ball, she decided to have tea served alfresco on the terrace. Wexford had promised her he would make a concerted effort to have the gentlemen back from their afternoon ride in time to take tea with the ladies.

As Clare moved about the terrace making sure her guests had been served and needed nothing further, she noted Viscount Hale vying for Violet's attention. He sat with her, being most attentive. Fortunately, her sister-in-law was on her best behavior and listened to whatever story the viscount was telling her as her eyes had not left his face.

"Do sit down and join us, Lady Clare," Her Grace the Duchess of Somerset said as she patted the cushion of a chair next to her. The duchess was the mother of Margaret Green, one of Violet's dear friends. The two families had become close over the years through their daughters' friendship.

"I really can't..."

"Nonsense, that's why you have staff. We'll all survive if you sit and enjoy a cup of tea," she replied, smiling at Clare.

Clare relented and sat next to the duchess. "You're right.

I suppose I'm obsessing because it's my first house party as Wexford's wife." She accepted a cup of tea the duchess poured for her. It wasn't proper for the duchess to pour, but Clare was thankful the woman felt so at ease.

"You're doing a marvelous job," the duchess replied.

"Thank you." She noted Violet and Margaret standing by the balustrade talking quite animatedly about something. One of the so-called suitors, she was sure.

"Lady Violet hasn't had a season?" Lady Benton observed. Her husband was a powerful man in Parliament and had recently inherited the earldom from his father. Lady Benton was an elegant woman with blond hair that showed no inclination toward turning gray, and a voluptuous figure even after all these years.

"No, though Wexford promised her one this year. I'm afraid my husband was too caught up in his newly inherited affairs and getting used to the fact that he now oversees four younger siblings."

"They're exhausting," the duchess said. She picked up her freshly poured cup of tea and looked thoughtfully at the two young women still talking at the edge of the terrace.

"Which is why I assume Lord Wexford invited a few of his bachelor friends," Lady Benton remarked with a smile on her well-preserved face.

"I know he had business to discuss with them, but I'm sure the thought crossed his mind when he invited them. You know how men do," Clare replied.

Lady Benton nibbled on a seed cake she had on her plate. "We were quite surprised when we learned Wexford had married, though seeing the two of you together, I can see it was a love match."

Clare laughed. "I know I certainly wasn't looking to marry. It has turned out to be far better than I expected."

"I understand Viscount Hale's looking for a wife. Did you know that?" Lady Benton asked Clare.

Clare, while not wanting to get into a discussion about the viscount and his fondness of younger ladies, decided it was best not to say too much.

"I believe Wexford may have mentioned it."

"He has grown daughters. Never had an heir. I suppose with his wife gone, he's decided to find another and try for a son," the duchess murmured.

"If he dies without an heir, I understand everything will be inherited by some obscure cousin," Clare said.

"Yes, and why not choose a younger woman with lots of childbearing years ahead of her," Lady Benton added.

Clare noted Violet seemed to be enjoying the viscount's attention immensely. She was laughing politely at something the older man had just said. Clare hoped it wasn't offensive. She wouldn't put it past the viscount to try to shock young ladies.

The other two younger men who had been invited had, for the most part, stayed out of the way when it came to the women. Clare wondered if they simply weren't interested or if they were being polite and waiting for festivities to begin.

Clare herself liked Phillip Marker, Marquess of Ashwood, as a match for Violet. He'd gone to Cambridge, and he had a sense of humor and was quite attentive to the fairer sex. Parr also had mentioned to her that the earl owned tin and coal mines and was comfortably wealthy. The tin mines around Cornwall had been most prosperous for Ashwood.

That left George Sutton, Viscount Alderbury. Out of these three men, Alderbury would be more in need of Violet's dowry. His father had just about ruined the family with his gambling and drinking. Though he was trying to establish himself apart from his father, it would be years before he showed any sort of measurable profit.

Though Clare tried not to judge the men for their financial stability, she was afraid with the marquess that he could possibly follow in his father's footsteps. Though Wexford had assured her he'd seen no such habits in Alderbury, she still wondered. Would he follow suit, and if he did, how long would it be before he fell victim to the drink and cards?

Clare stood and excused herself from the ladies' company. She needed to check on other guests and make sure preparations were underway for dinner. After-dinner activities this evening would include an immensely popular parlor game, charades. Afterward, the men could retire to the game room for billiards and the ladies could either retire or take tea in the drawing room.

She glanced over at Violet, who was still standing in the company of the viscount and her long-time friend. The girls seemed enthralled at some story the viscount was sharing. He was quite animated in his storytelling. Clare decided she would see if any of the men were to Violet's fancy. Violet was by nature overreactive and thrived on being the center of attention. Perhaps that was what he made her so vulnerable to the attentions of the Earl of Bath, or whomever the man was who had taken advantage of her naivete.

After an evening playing charades, Violet was invigorated. She had two suitors for sure. The Marquess of Ashwood had been a delightful partner this evening. With his vivid imagination, he'd been able to keep guests mystified at what they as a team were trying to convey.

Viscount Alderbury had bowed out after playing a

couple of rounds with her friend Margaret as his partner. Margaret had been disappointed, but he'd proved an amiable player nonetheless.

Though Viscount Hale had attended, he didn't participate, for which she was most grateful. The older gentleman had had a bit too much to drink in her opinion, and she didn't need a partner who was in his cups as deeply as Hale had been.

She was surprisingly intrigued by Hale. He was older, not at all handsome, but that could be to her advantage. He was well established in his business dealings and had mentioned to her more than once this day that he had to travel for business. That could be to her advantage as well, though she was sure she'd simply die if he touched her. The thought of sharing a marriage bed almost repulsed her, but a comment he'd made piqued her interest. He didn't need her dowry, and he would leave it with her. She would have access to it. In addition, she would receive pin money every quarter like she did now through Wexford.

"Oh, Jen! I simply can't make up my mind. Hale is most interested, but he's old and not at all attractive. Ashwood is so handsome and he's quite well-to-do, but then there's Alderbury. He's handsome, well-read, and has done well for himself, but he's barely paid me much attention. How do I choose?" Violet asked her younger sister as she flounced down on Jenny's bed while they were getting ready to retire.

"I would choose the marquess. He's handsome and witty. Hale would have his advantages, such as his frequently being out of town on business. But he's old, fat, and ugly."

"Jenny!"

"Well, you asked. As for the marquess, perhaps he's shy and needs some time alone to get to know you better."

"You're right. I hadn't thought that about Ashwood. I do

tend to be chatty, and the time hasn't presented itself for us to have much conversation," Violet replied.

Jenny's maid finished braiding her hair. "That's all for tonight," she said, then turned to Violet. "You know the marquess and his father, the Earl of Dunnwood are also friends of Parr's?"

"True. Hale, on the other hand, is a business acquaintance of our brother's."

"We're to go riding in the morning. Perhaps one of them will accompany you, if you know what I mean," Jenny replied.

"I'll tell you something, and you must keep it a secret. I'm liking Hale more and more. True, he's not at all pleasant to look at, but he's rich and he's made it clear my dowry would remain mine. He wouldn't be around all the time, so I'd be free to do more of what I want, like go to London and shop."

Jenny nodded thoughtfully. "I understand, but what about the other two?"

"They're friends with Wexford. Need I say more? Why, they'd probably give him a report on things that aren't any of Parr's business."

"I've heard the marquess has a temper," Jenny whispered.

"I have heard the same, but it might simply be that—a rumor. I imagine he's different in a personal relationship with a woman."

"Perhaps, but you should be aware of the rumor."

"I will keep that in mind."

"You must remember Viscount Hale wants more children. That seems to be his only reason for marriage, or his most imperative. He needs an heir, something his late wife was never able to have. A son. Do you want to be with child all the time, or until you bear him an heir? And if you did, wouldn't he then want another? A spare?"

"All valid points, sister. We'll see what tomorrow brings. I suppose I should get to bed. I imagine our new sister-in-law will want details should she come up to say good night."

"I'm glad Parr found her. It's nice to have another woman to discuss things like this with. Could you imagine talking to our brother about the virtue of his friends as marriage prospects?" Jenny laughed.

Violet shook her head. "It would never happen."

"Good night, sister. Let's hope one of them will speak with Parr in the next day or two."

"I hope so. I don't want a long courtship or engagement," she said. "Good night, Jenny."

Violet left her younger sister's room and got into her own bed. Yes, one of the men needed to speak with her brother, because she certainly didn't have the time to suffer a long courtship or engagement. That put Viscount Hale at the top of her list. He wouldn't want either himself. She would endure her wedding night, and as far as anyone would be concerned, she and the viscount would be expecting a child together. No one would think twice, since a son was the chief reason he was looking for such a young wife.

She still didn't know herself if she were with child. Her courses had ever been irregular but she had indulged in more than kisses with her lover. Her lover who had abandoned her. Even were she not with child, her dalliance could have repercussions, as in London, there had been rumors of her reckless behavior. The idea of living as a ruined woman held no appeal. This would be her best resolution to what could be a very embarrassing situation for not only her, but her family. She should never have believed that man when he told her he'd work everything out and leave his wife. He was a liar, and Violet knew she would rise above him and hoped he would eventually rot in hell. It was the least he deserved for putting her in such a predicament.

Besides, the viscount was old and wouldn't live forever, and when he did pass, she would be free to do all the things unattached or married women could not. Being a widow had its advantages.

She would try to get Wexford by himself tomorrow and find out if any of the gentlemen had approached him about courting her. Tomorrow night would be the soiree, and she couldn't wait to see how many of the available gentlemen would ask her for two dances. Anything more than two was scandalous, of course, but two dances would indicate to her that they were interested. Of course, if she could get one of them to take her for a stroll in the gardens, that would further tell of their intentions. Unless, of course, Wexford put word out that they weren't to be escorting his sister anywhere scandalous.

22

Wexford climbed into bed and turned to face Clare. She was breathtaking with her hair down and fanned across the pillow. She wore an ivory nightgown and smiled up at him as he settled in next to her. This is what made everything in life worthwhile. This woman for whom he would move heaven and earth. He wrapped his arms around her and drew her closer. She smelled faintly of lavender and honey.

"Hale and Ashwood both approached me about their wish to court my sister this evening," he said as he stroked her hair.

"What did they say? Better yet, how did you respond?"

"Ashwood is interested, but would like time to get reacquainted with her. If they rub along, he would like to be betrothed by summer's end, and marry before the end of the year."

"That's too long if Violet is indeed ruined and in need of marriage."

"Yes. Hale, on the other hand, would like to be married by special license. He doesn't need her dowry and is agreeable to setting it into a trust for any children they might have together."

Clare looked up at him. "The problem with Hale is his age. Violet needs to be taken care of."

"I mentioned that to him. Of course he thinks he'll live forever. He's willing to set aside funds for her and see that half her dowry is allocated to her upon his demise. She would be well taken care of."

"What about Alderbury? He's been quiet since he's been here and hasn't paid Violet much attention. From my own dealings with him, I find that suspicious."

"That's like him. He doesn't like to compete for a woman's affections, and I also think he's sitting back and watching what transpires with the other two."

"Could it be he's simply not interested in Violet?" she asked.

"That could very well be. We haven't had much chance to speak." He hesitated.

"What? Something bothers you," Clare said. Though they hadn't been married long, she already knew how to read his moods.

"To be perfectly honest, I don't feel right trying to match Violet with two of my closest friends, especially under the circumstances."

"I can respect that. Do you think Alderbury might suspect?"

He kissed the top of her head, still stroking her hair. "If he does, he's keeping it to himself. My friends have always assumed my sisters are unavailable, so my change of heart might have raised suspicions with him."

"Then I suppose we should let Hale pursue her, though I would hate to force Violet into a marriage in which she would be miserable," Clare replied.

"That would relieve my conscience."

"Well, we can't have you walking around feeling guilty, can we?"

"There's the girl I fell in love with."

She pulled back and threw him a pout. "Really?"

"Yes. You know I love it when you talk sassy."

"I'll have to remember that," she demurely replied.

He put his hand on her cheek and lifted her face to his and kissed her. "I hate to say it, but I must get up at dawn. The men and I are going hunting."

"Since when did that stop you?" she asked coyly.

"Since we have guests who must be entertained."

She arched a brow. "That's where I can honestly say being a woman has its advantages. Most of the women have their breakfast in bed. A few come to the breakfast room, but not nearly as early as you. So I can sleep a little longer."

He growled in her ear and loosened his grip on her. "A lady of leisure. Well, my dove, be prepared to get no sleep after our guests leave, as I intend to ravish you all night."

"Promises, promises, my lord. I look forward to the encounter," she teased.

She wiggled down in the bed, and Wexford held on to her. "I knew you might. Now, come, we need to get some sleep. Dawn will be here far too early."

"Are you taking Gregory and George with you?"

"Yes," he replied.

She had begun to fall asleep, and he wasn't sure if she heard his reply. That was fine; she was exhausted from the hours she'd been spending trying to be the perfect hostess. He was lucky to have found her. She had settled right into her role as his countess without hesitation, and from what he saw, everyone loved her. Then again, what was not to love about this lively, exquisite creature?

He pulled the covers tightly over both of them and lay there listening to her breathe until he succumbed to sleep himself. Little did he know that in a short time his bliss would be turned into a deep, mystical dream about someone few knew about, and those who did never spoke of: his long-departed cousin, Gideon Parr.

Gideon and Wexford often spent their summers together, with Gideon coming to Stratford. His mother had died giving birth to him, and the closest he'd ever had to a mother figure had been Wexford's own mother.

Every summer, he looked forward to Gideon's arrival, and every summer, they spent their time exploring the vast acreage available to them and hunting with his father. The two of them would ride across the meadows pretending to be crusaders or whatever adventure they managed to think up.

The tragedy happened the summer they were eight. The day had been like any other. They had decided to see how fast they could gallop their ponies to the border of the estate. Nothing unusual, except the day was somewhat overcast. As they got farther and farther away from the house, the more the sky seemed to darken.

Finally, the sky opened up and rain began to pour down in sheets. But on they continued as fast as they could. The ground became slippery, as the farthest area was bare since it had recently been replanted.

Wexford knew of a small, abandoned cottage near where they were headed and thought they might wait out the storm for a while before giving up and returning to the stables. First, however, they had to climb a small hill to where the cottage sat.

Regardless of the slick ground or the pelting rain, they both raced up the hill. Until Gideon's gelding stumbled, losing his balance and going onto his side. Gideon fell underneath the pony, and by the time the gelding regained his footing, it was obvious to Wexford that his cousin had been killed by the fall.

Gideon's gelding had bolted, heading back to the stables as fast as he could. Wexford wasn't strong enough to lift his cousin's lifeless body onto his own mount, so he sat with him in the rain until help finally arrived a couple of hours later.

The accident caused a rift between Gideon's father and Parr's father for a number of years. His uncle never came around as it was too painful. He blamed his brother, now the earl, for his son's death, for letting two young boys run wild and unsupervised. They eventually put their differences aside, but the closeness the two men had once shared was altered forever.

Wexford was moved out of the nursery and into another wing of the castle where he was separated from his siblings. His father hired the best tutors, and he spent his days learning Latin and French, literature, mathematics, and whatever else his father came up with. It was his way of punishing him. Wexford wasn't allowed to take meals with his siblings or leave his new rooms. He was a virtual prisoner—at least it felt like that to an eight-year-old boy.

Now he realized how an accident had helped to destroy several close relationships, when it had been just that: an accident. Thoughts of Gideon evoked a memory of Matilda, and he realized as he lay there in the quiet night that her death had been an accident as well, and he was not to blame. He'd nearly let his guilt over her death stop him from seeking love again. Perhaps Gideon had sent him the dream as a message. Or perhaps he was simply happy again, and grateful, and knew finally he should lay his guilty conscience to rest.

One of these days, he would tell Clare and possibly his younger siblings about him, but for now, he preferred keeping some things private. Alexandria, of course, would probably remember Gideon, but being a girl a couple of years older than he, her mind was on more feminine pursuits. His father would have shielded her, and the time he'd spent locked away as punishment was never discussed between them. He doubted his sister truly understood the circumstances or if she even remembered.

He turned to face Clare, who lay peacefully sleeping. She looked as though she hadn't a care in the world, and that was the way he meant to keep it. Once this party was over, and if Violet had made her choice, he would make sure Clare had time to do something for herself. She'd taken all the children coming to live with them for the summer in stride, and as far as he could tell, they adored her. Violet, of course, was always another story, but it seemed as though she and Clare had formed some sort of mutual under-standing between them.

Deciding he needed to try to get back to sleep, he closed his eyes and said a silent prayer for Gideon and Matilda.

He tucked himself up against Clare's backside and wrapped an arm around her. She barely moved except to burrow against his chest and manly parts with her backside. He smiled as his eyes grew heavy, knowing he was the luckiest man alive.

WHEN CLARE WOKE UP, PARR'S SIDE OF THE BED WAS EMPTY and cold, though she could still smell his musky masculine scent. The blazing fire took any chill out of the room. She lay there for a moment longer. Today was going to be busy with all the preparations for the party this evening. Even with her staff having everything under control, Clare couldn't help but assist. It was their first social event as a married couple, and she wanted it to be perfect.

Parr had been restless all night. She remembered him finally getting up once and standing in front of the smoldering fire. She'd thought to get up and make sure he was all right, but she fell back to sleep herself and had slept through the remainder of the night.

"Good morning, my lady. Would you like to bathe this morning or wait until later this afternoon?" Agnes asked as she pulled back the draperies, revealing the sunshine.

"I think I'll wait until this afternoon. I plan to help with any last-minute details in between hosting the ladies."

"Did you have anything in mind for the ladies today?"

"A picnic in the rose garden might be nice. It wouldn't require much walking, and would be easier to get to than the meadow near the river."

"I'm sure the ladies will appreciate that and enjoy it immensely," Agnes replied.

Clare headed behind the screen to do her toilette. She glanced at her lady's maid. "I never knew hosting a house party could be so exhausting."

A short while later, Clare was ready to go to the breakfast room when Violet came flouncing through the door and flung herself on the bed.

"I'm so nervous! You have no idea!" the girl exclaimed.

"Yes, I'm sure."

Violet rolled her eyes. "No, you don't. My life is in the balance. It will forever change after tonight."

"Only if that's what you want," Clare replied.

"What does my brother say? Who is he in favor of? The old viscount or one of the young bucks? And please, spare me the boring details about money and property."

"He hasn't really said. I only know that he wants to be sure you are taken care of if you were to marry the viscount. If he proposes marriage, that is."

"I would think he would do that regardless of who it was," Violet sniffed.

"It's different with the viscount. He's older. There are many variables, and Parr wants to make sure they're all taken into account," Clare replied. "But come, let's go to breakfast. We needn't worry about such matters."

"You're right. There's nothing for us to do now. I'm starving, so let's go eat."

"Let's. I noticed you didn't eat much last night."

The breakfast room was void of any other ladies, for which Clare was thankful. There was too much to do and Clare thought it a waste of time to lounge around in bed if she wasn't ill.

She and Violet took their seats. She poured them a cup of tea as they waited on a footman to bring them each a plate of eggs, toast, and sausages.

"Would you truly be happy with Hale?" Clare asked Violet, who was adding honey to her tea.

"I would be once I bore him a son. That's all he wants. After that, we could live our lives as we wished."

"But what if he didn't want that? What if he expected you to continue to put on a happy face in front of others and live as man and wife? Could you do it?"

Violet stirred her tea vigorously as she thought this through. "You mean share a marital bed after the deed of giving him a child is completed? Absolutely not," she replied. "Why do you ask? Has Parr said something?"

"No, he hasn't. I was curious because the viscount is older and set in his ways. His thoughts regarding marriage, I'm sure, could never be changed. You'd have to be willing to live as he expects."

"How's that?"

Clare arched a brow. "As his obedient wife."

"No! I will not be some man's property."

"You know that's how most men see women. As their property."

They both sat back as a footman delivered two plates, one in front of each of them. Clare could tell from the expression on Violet's face that she was furious. She smiled to herself. Perhaps her young sister-in-law was beginning to see the reality of getting married. Most were negotiated deals, deals made by men. Few men ever took a woman's needs or feelings into consideration when pounding out marriage contracts.

"But Parr doesn't treat you as property or as if you're some half-wit."

Clare almost smiled at Violet's comment, but didn't. "That's because he doesn't feel that way, and because we love each other."

"But can you marry based on mutual respect and hope it grows into love? Not all arranged marriages are horrid, are they?"

"Yes, time changes many things, and no, not all arranged marriages are fraught with animosity or are cold and distant."

"Do you think I'm making a mistake with Hale?"

"Let me ask you this first. Can you see yourself spending the rest of your days with him? I doubt he's going to let you go live with your child on one of his estates. Not when he can parade his new young wife around London."

"I hadn't thought of that. I merely assumed he wasn't the type who would want a wife attending him all the time."

Clare shook her head. "You're young and beautiful, Violet. What man wouldn't want a wife as attractive as you on their arm?"

"What am I going to do, Clare?" she asked despairingly.

Clare looked around to make sure they were alone. Usually once she and Wexford were served, the servant left the room, thus ensuring they had some privacy to talk.

"Parr and I will help you any way possible, you know that. Your brother would rather you remain unmarried than miserable. He's not one of those men who has to marry his sister off like a business transaction," she replied. "Your feelings matter to him as well, but be aware that if you decide to remain unmarried, the ton will shun you should word leak out about your condition. Can you tell me how you were compromised, Violet? It might make all the difference in the world."

The girl looked at her despairingly. "We did..." She hesitated. "He did... My courses have not resumed," she said at last, eyes downcast. Does anyone know? I mean besides you and Parr?"

Clare felt her heart sink. "No, but people are going to speculate. If you marry one of these men in haste, people will wonder, especially when the child is born seven months after you marry. Should you decide to retire to one of your brother's other estates, the ton will wag their tongues, though I do have an idea to prevent that from following you."

"What do you have in mind?"

"Your great aunt Mary. She lives on the estate outside Oxfordshire. You could go there to be her companion."

"And then never marry at all?" With a sad shake of her

head, Violet pushed her empty plate in front of her and finished the last of her tea. "Thank you, Clare. You've given me much to think about." She rose from her chair. "Do you need me to help with anything?"

"No, I believe I have everything in hand. You go enjoy the day. I'll be here if you need me."

She nodded before leaving the room. Clare breathed a sigh of relief. Perhaps she'd given her young sister-in-law enough information to make an informed decision. Whatever choice she made would change her life forever.

The house was quite a sight to behold when Wexford and Clare descended the stairs that evening. Candles glowed from windows and throughout the grand hall. Flowers from the gardens were placed in vases on tables scattered throughout as well.

They joined Gregory and George, along with his two sisters, Jenny and Violet, to form a reception line. They were all old enough to begin using the social skills they'd been taught all these years.

"Everyone looks quite handsome or pretty," Clare whispered to him.

This was the first time he'd allowed them to be part of anything with adults. Except for Violet, they would all excuse themselves after a short period of time after guests had been greeted. He certainly hoped Violet attracted one of the young men or Viscount Hale enough for one of them to offer marriage. None except Hale and Ashwood had approached him, but that didn't make Wexford concerned.

Hale was overdoing things; he was most anxious to take a new wife, one who would give him an heir. He and

Ashwood had briefly discussed the matter, but it was Hale pushing his interest among other things. Viscount Alderbury had shown no interest, but perhaps that would all change this evening. He would keep an eye on all three and Violet to see if he could tell if any attachments were forming.

They went through the motions of the receiving line, introducing his siblings and wife.

His wife looked delicious. She wore an emerald-green silk gown, her hair swept up off her neck, letting the choker of pearls he'd given her earlier this evening become the focal point. She displayed herself with grace and ease. He could not have chosen a better woman to be his wife.

"Have I told you how beautiful you look this evening, my love?" he asked after they finished greeting the last of the guests.

She smiled warmly at him. "At least twice, but please, don't stop. I love hearing your compliments."

"And I'll never stop, my dove," he replied. "I suppose we should go in and start the first set."

"I'm ready when you are, my lord," she murmured as she placed her hand on his forearm. Together, they walked into the ballroom where the orchestra was warming up. Wexford nodded to the leader as he and Clare took their places. The music began, and he led her through the first of the elaborate steps of a cotillion as they had planned. Plenty of country reels and waltzes would follow later. Clare had wanted to have a good mix for their guests, and even though he didn't particularly like to dance, Wexford agreed with his bride on this particular matter.

As couples joined them, he noticed his sister Violet was paired up with Alderbury. Odd, since his old friend hadn't had much to say about her. Wexford had seen them together on several occasions, but didn't believe there was anything but a friendship developing.

"Alderbury?" Clare asked as they left the dance floor. "I thought he wasn't interested."

"I believe he's simply humoring me, that's all. Being polite. I don't see anything more than a friendship between them, if that. I'm afraid she thinks he's tedious and boring."

Clare nodded. "Yes, and we both know Violet has a flare for the dramatic."

He grinned, his eyes on his wife. "Yes, she does."

"I know you need to do whatever it is you gentlemen do at these affairs. I need to speak with a couple of the ladies from neighboring estates."

"Very well. Save the first waltz for me," he replied. "I think it's time for Jenny and the boys to retire for the night. I'll speak with them if you wish."

"I'll get Jenny; you handle George and Gregory. They think they're too old to spend the evening in the nursery, and will be more willing to leave if it comes from you."

He nodded, bowed, and strode toward his two brothers, while Clare found Jenny engaged in a conversation with her sister's friend, Lady Margaret.

Wexford hated getting caught up in business or political discussions, but aside from cards and dancing or dining with their wives, this was how men spent most of their time at affairs like this. He would rather be with Clare, or even standing at the side of the ballroom observing his sister Violet. He hoped by the end of the evening, there might be one young man who caught her fancy.

The Earl of Dunnwood, William Marker, whose estate ran to the north of his, neared Wexford. "Dunnwood, it's good to see you. Your man wasn't sure you'd arrive in time for this soiree."

"Got back late last night. Good to see you as well. I take it your lovely bride is busy with the ladies," he replied.

"Yes, and keeping an eye on my sister Violet."

"Phillip already found her," the earl replied. Phillip was his oldest son, the Marquess of Ashwood. Violet and the marquess had grown up together and still saw each other whenever Phillip came home from Eton. "The last I saw, he was signing her dance card and talking with her."

"I forgot they knew each other so well."

Dunnwood leaned in closer. "When you have some time, I thought to run a business idea by you that I came up with while I was away. It would benefit us both."

"You've got my attention." Wexford nodded. "Let's plan to sit down in the next few days. I'd hate for someone to overhear your idea."

"Excellent," he replied. He gazed about the room as though looking for someone. "I thought I saw Hale when I first arrived."

"Yes, he's here."

"You know he's looking for a wife, a young wife. Needs to have a son for the usual reasons."

Wexford smiled. "Yes, I'd heard. He's voiced his interest in Violet."

Dunnwood looked appalled. "Please don't tell me you're seriously considering him."

"No."

"Good. He's much too old for Violet, not to mention he has a few vices I wouldn't want my sister to have to marry into."

Wexford arched a brow. "I don't want her married to someone like him. I don't wish her to be miserable, and she would be with Hale. Whom are you suggesting I consider for Violet? Your son? You're putting Phillip forward as a potential suitor?"

"Pish—Phillip is far too young to marry at present. He needs a year or two to grow into his role as marquess. Perhaps, however, we might discuss an arrangement. I can assure you it would be far more beneficial than, say, Hale could offer."

"Come, let me pour you a drink," Wexford told Dunnwood as he led his neighbor and friend to a mahogany table filled with various crystal decanters. An arranged marriage would never work, not if Violet were truly with child. She couldn't afford to wait a few years. He hadn't seen the earl's son in a couple of years, due to his schedule or the boy's schooling. An arranged marriage between the young man and Jenny might more to both their benefits.

They stood and drank a glass of whiskey, and were about to get themselves in the midst of a matter before Parliament when Wexford remembered he'd promised Clare the first waltz.

"Come, let me introduce you to my wife." He leaned over closer to the earl. "I promised her the first waltz, and since this is our first social event since we married, I'd best join her."

"Yes, I'm sure Lady Alice would like a turn around the dance floor as well."

CLARE GLANCED OVER AT HER SISTER-IN-LAW, WHO WAS waltzing with the older viscount and looking miserable. At least to her, she looked unhappy. But then Violet was extremely good at masking her feelings from anyone who wasn't in her inner circle—her family.

"Who are you watching, my love?" she heard Parr whisper in her ear. "Violet can take care of herself with Hale."

"Can she?" she replied. "She seemed to have a wonderful rapport with young Lord Ashwood, more than she has any of the others."

"Ashwood is a neighbor. They grew up together, spent many a summer in each other's company."

"Yes, well, he wouldn't do, would he?" Clare said teasingly.

"Under the circumstances? No. His father believes he needs to have some time to grow. I agree."

"Drat."

"All is not lost, my love. I'll explain later, in the privacy of our bedchamber."

She smiled in his direction. "I like the sound of that."

When the dance was finished, Clare let her husband lead her to a group of older ladies who were sitting together. Before she joined them, she looked across the room for Violet and found her talking with Hale before he led her onto the terrace. She lost her breath as she watched them. The viscount was being quite animated with her. Was he going to ask her to marry him?

Though the terrace had a number of couples walking around, her sister-in-law knew better than to let him lead her to the gardens. The gardens were well lit, but still, if someone like Hale was that determined, he might try to compromise Violet in order to make sure they'd marry.

"You've got your hands full with that one," Lady Alice mused. "Lady Violet has always had quite the flair for the dramatic."

"Yes," Clare agreed, "she loves being the center of attention. She wears me out some days."

"I'm surprised the earl would encourage anything between the viscount and Lady Violet."

Clare calmed herself before speaking. She had to remember only she and Parr knew what was actually going on here. All one of Violet's little plays. "Lady Violet is merely being gracious to her brother's friends and associates. Like you said, the girl has always had a flair for the dramatic."

The viscount and Violet walked to the edge of the terrace. She turned to face the countess. "You must come for tea one afternoon."

"I would love to," Lady Alice replied. "Have you met Father Gray yet, or had the chance to shop in the village? It's really quite quaint, though you don't have the variety one gets in London."

"I met the vicar briefly one day when I took the girls to shop for ribbons. You're right, it's quaint, but even if the shops don't compare to London, they suffice."

The two women rejoined a small group of ladies as Clare kept a watchful eye on the open French doors, waiting for Violet to return.

A new dance set began, and couples paired up for the country dance to begin. Not seeing Violet anywhere, Clare began to get nervous. She knew Violet's dance card was full, so where was she? Surely Hale hadn't absconded with her into a dark corner of the gardens, had he?

She was about to find Wexford when a voice whispered in her ear. "Lady Wexford, have you seen Lady Violet? This is our dance, and I can't seem to find her anywhere."

The voice belonged to the Alderbury, who had spent most of his time since arriving either avoiding Violet or having polite conversation with her, always in the presence of others.

"No, I'm afraid I haven't. I was about to go out to the terrace to look as the last time I saw her, she was headed out there. With Viscount Hale."

"Would you like for me to take a look for you?" he asked.

Just then, Violet walked through the door. Clare could tell something wasn't right, but whatever it was Violet wasn't going to allow whatever it was ruin her evening. She made her way quickly across the room to them.

"That won't be necessary, my lord. Here she comes now," Clare replied.

"Lord Alderbury, I believe this is our dance," she said with a gracious smile.

"Shall we?" He offered his arm, and the pair found their way to the middle of the floor where the dance was just beginning.

Clare breathed a sigh of relief and watched for any sign of distress on her sister-in-law. She hadn't seen the viscount reappear either. She glanced at the door and then back at the dancers, where finding Alderbury and Violet was difficult as they were on the opposite side of the room. Couples whirled by until the pair appeared. They seemed to be enjoying each other's company. Whatever the young viscount had said to Violet had caused her to laugh and play coy.

She wondered why Ashwood didn't appear interested in Violet. Perhaps he was just that, uninterested in her other than a friend. Did he have another, someone he hadn't introduced anyone to? Or more likely, had he simply seen through the façade and was keeping a respectful distance? As long as Violet was happy with her choice that was all that mattered. If things had happened any other way, she might have encouraged a match between them, but they were running out of time.

She had faith in Violet. Though she was theatrical and self-absorbed, she did have a good heart. After all, people forgot Wexford and his siblings had been left without their parents, and Violet had been at a young, vulnerable age. Clare always thought this was why Violet acted as she did. She was protecting her heart.

Finally, the evening came to an end. Clare and Wexford had said good night to their departing guests or those staying with them. "I think your party was a smashing success," Wexford said, leading her back into the house after the last carriage departed.

"Our party," she reminded him. "And yes, I think it went well."

"So far, only Hale has asked to court Violet. Perhaps in the morning, one of the younger men will come forward.."

Clare nodded. "Speaking of Hale, I haven't seen him for a while." She didn't want to mention the viscount escorting Violet onto the terrace nor her troubled expression when she returned.

"I believe he's retired for the evening."

"Which is exactly what I suggest we do," she said demurely.

"Let me make sure the gentlemen have all retired, and then I'll join you," he replied quietly.

"Don't take too long, my lord. I'm not sure how long I can hold my head up," she teased as he left her at the bottom of the staircase.

"Just a little longer, my dove. I have plans for us tonight."

She tossed him a saucy look and began up the stairs, holding her skirts just high enough for him to get a good glimpse of what delights were underneath.

After sharing a quick drink with two remaining gentlemen who hadn't retired, Wexford opened the door to the bedchamber he shared with his wife. The only light in the room was the waning flames flickering from the fire which had been made to warm the room from the cooler English nights.

He glanced toward the bed and found her emerald-green eyes following his every move. Rich ginger hair was splayed across the pillows, the covers hiding any trace of her body. He was intrigued. He moved closer, shrugged out of his jacket and cravat. His shirt quickly followed. He sat on the bed and began to remove his boots and socks. Wexford felt a warm hand touch his lower back.

"Parr," she whispered.

He stood, unfastened his pants, and pulled them off. He lifted the covers and gathered Clare in his arms. This was heaven; this was what love was really about.

She licked her lips in naughty anticipation.

"Clare," he whispered.

"Kiss me."

Her wish was his to fulfill. He pressed his hands to her cheeks, pulling her mouth against his for a long, torrid kiss. One of his hands moved to her naked hip and cupped her bottom. There was no space between them as she lay on her back, his body pressed hard against hers.

"I want you," she said as she looked into his eyes when he lifted his head.

"And you shall have me," he growled.

His hands were everywhere, as were his lips.

"Dear God, Parr," she gasped as he slid a finger into her damp passage. Her hips bucked and arched, trying to get closer.

He moved over her and felt her legs slide open as his body nestled between them. His mouth trailed along her neck to the hollow of where her shoulder and neck joined.

She jerked beneath him as he slid his finger deep one last time before removing the digit and replacing it with his hot, swollen cock.

They found their rhythm, which became more intense with each passing moment.

"Please, harder," she begged. "Please..."

He remembered calling out her name. He moaned and slipped a hand between their bodies. She grabbed at him, her hands pressed into his shoulders. He felt her back arch as he claimed her for his own, her body shuddering under him. He let go, and their world exploded around them.

"I love you," he gasped. He collapsed on top of her, then kissed her and drew her close.

"That," she said, "was amazing."

"I'm glad you approved, my dove."

"Will it always be like this?" she asked quietly.

His grip tightened around her. "It will if I have any say about it."

She kissed his chest, running her fingers through the patch of dark blond hair on his chest. "Do you think you're up for another go?"

"What, now?"

"Yes, now," she teased.

"Hmmm, I suppose I could be persuaded, but only if you let me set the pace."

"We'll see, but this time, I'm in charge."

She sat up quickly and pushed him onto his back. She covered him, his cock ready for her, Slowly, she impaled herself on him, watching him closely. Clare ran her hands through her hair before she began to tease him. He had begun to slowly withdraw his cock, preparing himself for the next. Suddenly she pushed down, his cock impaled her as far as it could. And then she ground her hips against his, almost causing him to lose control.

"What are you up to, minx?"

She repeated what they'd just done together; this time, she stopped and stared down at him. "There is something I need to tell you, and this seemed the most private way to get that done."

"Whatever it is, you couldn't have picked a more intimate time," he rasped.

"I love you, Parr. With all my heart. I thank God every day for having brought you to me."

His eyes widened. "I love you too, my dove."

"With everything that's been going on around here. I wanted the most private time I could think of to tell you more than a simple I love you," she replied.

He held her hips and began to make love to her. "You have no idea how happy you've made me. I love you. With all my heart." He stopped after pushing deep inside her. "Should we be doing this? Is it safe for the babe?"

"As long as I'm not in discomfort, I can do whatever I wish, though I can't imagine you wanting to make love to me when I'm as huge as a house."

"I'll take you any way I can get you, Countess."

"The only thing I do ask is that we wait to share our news until we know what exactly Violet intends to do. Let's wait and see which gentleman she's chosen. If she has indeed chosen any."

"Agreed," he replied. "Now, one more thing, my love."

"What is that?"

"We must finish what we've started here."

She twined her arms around his neck. "Yes..."

The night was theirs, at least for a while. Afterward, as

they fell asleep in the glow of their lovemaking, others were continuing with their plans.

Wexford sat writing at a small desk in the sitting room adjoining their bedchamber. Guests would be leaving today, the house would be abuzz with activity. He used the quiet of their chambers to take care of personal correspondence.

Someone knocked on the door quite frantically. What could possibly be so urgent?

He buttoned up his shirt and walked across the room. When he opened the door, there stood Jenny, dressed in nothing but her nightgown and robe in her bare feet. She looked panicked.

"Good morning, my lord. I hate to interrupt, but I must see my sister."

Wexford swung open the door and invited her in. "Clare is still in bed, but awake, I believe," he said. "What is wrong, Jenny?"

"Yes, what is wrong, sister?" Clare asked as she appeared through the bedchamber door. She'd managed to dress, though she had no stockings or shoes on yet.

"It…it's Violet," she said breathlessly. "She's nowhere to be found. Her room is empty. Her bed wasn't slept in."

Clare glanced his way. Wexford nodded to her, then quietly left the room.

"Come," she said to Jenny. "I'm sure she's merely gone for an early morning ride. She was probably too excited from the party. Parr is likely making inquiries of the staff as we speak." She touched Jenny gently on the shoulder. "Why don't you dress? I'll meet you in the breakfast room. By then, Wexford will join me. Perhaps he'll have word."

Young Jenny headed out the door. When the door had closed behind her, Clare leaned up against it. What had Violet done? Where was she?

She went to put on her stockings and boots, in case she needed to go outside. As she was finishing, Wexford strode back into the bedchamber.

"Did you get Jenny calmed?" he asked her.

"Yes, she's gone to dress. I told her to meet me in the breakfast room."

He nodded, his expression grim. "Guests may be there as well, so I came here to tell you what I found out when I went to the stables. Violet and Phillip went for a ride at dawn this morning."

"Phillip Marker, the Marquess of Ashwood, the Earl of Dunnwood's son?"

"Yes. He also brought his carriage. Told the stable master he wanted the wheelwright in the village to look at one of the wheels. The carriage left for the village after Ashwood and Violet had left on their ride."

"Nothing sounds out of the ordinary there," Clare replied. "I suppose we must wait for them to return. Are you ready for breakfast?"

"Yes. We must keep our suspicions to ourselves, even from the children."

"What do we suspect?"

"Perhaps Ashwood and Violet are more interested in each other than they're letting on," he replied, guiding her to the door. "Come, let's go downstairs. Guests are leaving, and I would like to keep this as quiet as possible until we have a better grasp of what is going on."

As they neared the breakfast room door, Viscount Hale approached Wexford. His face was unreadable, but Wexford could tell the effort was almost more than Hale could express. He'd been waiting for Hale to request a formal meeting about a betrothal to Violet. Or had he heard about her having gone off alone with the Marquess of Ashwood?

"Good morning, Hale," he said curtly, leading Clare to the door.

"Wexford, a moment of your time."

"Now? Can't it wait until after I have breakfast, or at least a cup of tea?"

"It cannot wait," he replied.

Wexford glanced at his wife and nodded to her, telling her to go on without him. "Very well, shall we go to my study. We can speak more privately there."

The doors closed behind them as they entered Wexford's study. He beckoned the viscount to take a seat in front of the fire. He led the way, sitting in a leather wingback chair facing the fire.

"I imagine you wish to speak about a betrothal to my sister Violet?"

"Yes. The sooner the better. If we're in agreement, I'll obtain a special license. We can be married in a fortnight."

Wexford arched a brow. "What about the details of her dowry, the marriage?"

"I'm sure we can work them out after I have your blessing and have informed Lady Violet," the viscount replied. "There are too many young bucks sniffing around her. In fact, I hear she went riding with Lord Ashwood."

"I'm afraid I can't hand my sister over like she's a brood-mare. I understand your need for an heir, but Lady Violet is a vibrant young woman. She needs to be treated with respect, and if you don't understand that, Hale...in fact, I'll wait on an answer until I've had a chance to speak with Lady Violet alone. If she's in agreement, I'll send for you and I'll talk with the two of you together."

He could tell the viscount didn't like the way things were going. The man had been quite sure he'd walk in here and leave knowing Violet was going to be his wife. "As you wish, my lord."

He heard the door slam behind the viscount, who had obviously not waited for a footman. This would give Wexford time to find out what was going on with his sister, and he liked the idea to include Violet in the discussion regarding marriage to the viscount. The man wanted her because she was young and would hopefully give him many sons. He would rather be there when she refused Hale because Wexford had the feeling if she did it alone, Hale wouldn't take the rebuff like a gentleman.

Returning to the breakfast room, he noted it had cleared out. Clare was with guests heading back home. The only person remaining was young Jenny, who was in the midst of piling marmalade on a piece of toast.

"I'm looking into things."

"I know you are," she replied without looking up from her plate.

"But? You have doubts?"

"No, of course not."

"Tell me what's on your mind, Jenny."

She looked up, licking her thumb. "You don't think the marquess would take her off to marry him, do you? Assuming she and the marquess return from their ride."

She had made a valid point. One he hadn't considered.

"Your sister will be fine, trust me. You can't believe she would let Lord Phillip abscond with her. Besides, they've been friends for years. No one can make Violet do what she doesn't want to do."

She giggled. "She does like to be theatrical, doesn't she? I can hear her now."

"Yes, she does," he agreed. He sat back to let the footman place a plate filled with eggs, toast, and meats in front of him.

He leaned forward and cut some ham. "What are you about today?"

"I don't know. I thought I might paint outside once all the guests have left."

"Would you care to ride with me? I would like to survey the cattle."

"Oh yes, I would," she said excitedly.

"Then finish your breakfast and go change into a riding outfit. I'll have a horse readied for you."

She nodded. Usually, he spent time with his brothers. Now, with Violet possibly marrying, Jenny would be the only one left at home once the boys left for Eton.

Soon, she would be presented and have her first season. She was growing up too fast, too soon. Perhaps he needed to find her a husband, an arranged marriage.

"What are you smiling at?" Jenny asked as she rose from her chair.

"Nothing, nothing at all. Shall we meet in the hall, say in an hour?"

She grinned. "Perfect." Jenny sprinted to the door.

He'd finished his breakfast and was glancing over the newspapers as he sipped his second cup of tea when Clare came rushing in, the butler following behind her.

"A letter just arrived," Clare said breathlessly.

The butler presented the tray and took the folded paper. He studied it momentarily. It was in Violet's hand. "Thank you," he said. "That'll be all."

He held it until the door shut behind the servants. They were alone in the room. "Should I open it or wait until all the guests have left?"

"Now, Parr! All our guests have left. Even Hale, and he huffed out of here and mumbled something about telling you he'd be in touch with you about a further meeting regarding Violet."

"I knew he wouldn't give up that easily," he said as he broke the seal.

His eyes scanned the contents. He smiled and handed it to Clare.

Parr,

By the time you get this, Ashwood and I will be well on our way to Gretna Green.

Please don't try to stop us. I have told him all, and he is eager to marry me, as I am him. I am quite happy and look forward to sharing our adventures with you sometime soon. Will write as soon as we've settled. Ashwood wishes to take me on a wedding trip.

Your loving sister -
Violet

"Well, well, well," Clare said. "The one with whom she's most comfortable is the one she chooses. How long do you think they've been playing this game with us?"

"I have no idea," Parr replied. "I imagine they've been playing us all along."

Clare arched a brow and stared down at her husband. "You're not going to stop them, are you?"

He shook his head. "No. She's Ashwood's problem now."

"Yet the fact that she told him of her potential condition is a good sign. Perhaps Violet is maturing from the headstrong girl she was."

"Indeed. She has managed to find her own solution to her predicament. Yet if he'd refused her..."

"Let's not dwell on that and just be happy for them. They aren't the only ones who eloped to Gretna Green, after all." Clare blushed, Parr had to chuckle.

He rose from his chair and handed the letter to her. "Put this somewhere private. We'll discuss the matter further later."

"Where are you off to?"

He grinned. "Riding with my youngest sister. I have a feeling an arranged marriage is looming in Jenny's future, and I should like to spend more time with her."

"Yes, without Violet, she's going to be lonely."

He kissed her gently on the lips. "You need to rest while we're gone. The boys are off being boys and the guests have left. Enjoy your time."

"I love you, Parr."

"And I love you, my heart. Always. Through thick and thin and siblings galore, you're the most important thing in my life."

She smiled at his loving words. "Go, before Jenny comes looking for you. You know how she adores spending time with you."

He nodded. "I am looking forward to things quieting down."

She smiled as he turned and walked off. Things certainly wouldn't be quiet any time soon. Her husband had far too many younger siblings for things to be anything but quiet and calm, and she adored it.

Clare paused to wonder how Violet was, and where she was. How had the two of them managed to have kept their feelings for the other to themselves? No one had suspected at thing.

She heard commotion in the entry hall. It sounded like the Earl of Dunnwood, Ashwood's father. From the tone of his voice, he was not happy.

The butler, stoic as ever, entered the room. "The Earl of Dunnwood would like a word with you. I told him Lord Wexford was out riding and unavailable."

"That's fine. I'll see him. Please put the earl in the red drawing room. I'll be there momentarily."

The butler bowed before leaving. "As you wish, madam."

Clare was sure the duke had been left a letter similar to the one Parr had received. The problem with Ashwood's father was that he thought his son needed to get some worldly experience before settling down and marrying. She wasn't at all sure that might include a marriage to Lady Violet.

She didn't hesitate when the footman opened the door to the drawing room. The earl stood facing the French doors that overlooked the gardens.

"My lord," she began. "I apologize, but my husband has gone riding. I was told it was urgent that you see him. I hope I'll do for a substitute for now."

The earl turned, eyes blazing. "I'm sure you've received a letter such as this," he said, waving a piece of paper in the air.

"Yes, we received one from Violet."

"Did you know this was going on? That my son and Wexford's sister were secretly keeping company?"

Clare motioned for the man to sit, but he was having none of it. He stood stolidly in front of the fire. "We were just as shocked as you. We had no idea."

"I find that difficult to believe."

"Find what difficult to believe, my lord?"

"That no one knew of this."

Clare shook her head. "Wexford was speechless."

"Well, this will not happen. I'll have this sham of a marriage annulled as soon as they return. No son of mine is going to ruin his life."

Clare stared at him. "Are you accusing Lady Violet of something, my lord? Because if you are, tread lightly. They've chosen to go to Gretna Green. I'm afraid there is nothing that can be done to stop it. You know that as well as I."

"He is my heir. I expected him to wait until he was ready."

"Obviously, he thought differently."

"Yes, but he is my legacy..."

"Who has nothing but love and admiration for you," Clare replied.

The earl nodded and turned to face Clare. "You're right, of course," he replied. "I've taken up enough of your time. Please tell your husband I'll speak with him soon."

"Of course."

The man bowed and quit the room. She couldn't help but notice he appeared to have aged a great deal since receiving the news. Time and circumstances had a way of changing one, and not even an earl was immune to what life dealt a person. It mattered only how that person chose to accept or refuse it.

Parr found his wife doing needlework near the fire in the drawing room. She barely looked up from her work as he approached.

"You had a nice ride? Your sister behaved?"

"Yes, to both your questions," he replied. He kissed her on the cheek and, hands behind his back, stood in front of the chair. "I understand we had a visitor while I was out."

"Yes, the Earl of Dunnwood. He received a letter from the marquess about his and Violet's sudden trip to Gretna Green."

Parr smiled. "And what was his mood?"

"Furious at first. He obviously had his son's life all laid out."

"Yes, he did. I take it you were able to calm the earl?"

"I believe so. By the time he left, he was resigned to the fact there was nothing he could do if this was what his son chose."

Parr arched a brow. "That doesn't sound like Dunnwood."

"He did appear distressed by the news," Clare offered.

"He'll come around, or perhaps he's already resigned himself to the fact, as you said."

"The earl said he'd speak with you another time."

"Very well," he replied. "I thought you were going to lie down and rest for a while?"

"I haven't had an opportunity, but I'm fine. It's been quiet, and I'm enjoying sitting here. With you now."

"Yes, well, I'm afraid I must go work in my study for a couple of hours. I've been a bit lax what with all the guests and goings on."

"I understand, and if I'm not here when you finish, I'll be in our bedchamber."

He smiled wickedly, neared, and took her hand, kissing the back. "I think the bedchamber will allow you far better rest than here, my heart."

"I look forward to it, my lord."

He left and headed toward his study. There was much to do, catching up from where he allowed himself to be distracted by the house party. He normally didn't do that, but this hadn't been regular circumstances. The sooner he got it all done, the sooner he could spend some much-needed quiet time with Clare. From an unlikely courtship to the love that continued to grow and flourish with each passing day, he was content. Content with his life and all that it encompassed.

Soon, they would welcome their first child, and with any luck, that child would be a boy. His heir, the next generation to inherit the earldom when it came time. Life was more than good; it was perfect, and he couldn't wait for the next phase life had to offer.

A child was on the way. Hopefully an heir, and with him a new generation of Parrs. The future Earl of Wexford.

EPILOGUE

Ten months later, Lady Violet strolled through the door at Wexford Castle on the arm of her husband, Phillip Marker, Marquess of Ashwood. She looked radiant and happier than her brother could ever remember.

Ashwood was smiling as he watched her family's reaction to the babe fast asleep in his nurse's arms. The true daughter of Phillip and Violet, much to Clare and Parr's relief.

Lady Beatrice Violet Clare Marker had made her entrance into the world with as much noise as she could muster, and as dramatic as her mother, staring at those around her with chocolate-brown eyes.

Parr and Clare's infant son was fast asleep in the nursery at the moment. Thinking of his darling child, Wexford stood next to his countess, his hand on her barely swelled belly, their second on the way, smiling as he greeted his younger sister and her dashing husband.

But that's a story for another time.

ALSO BY JAMIE SALISBURY

Mayfair

Dealing with the Duchess

Ravaging the Duke

To Love An Earl

The Marquess Takes A Bride

MacLeods of Skye

Donnan's Rose

The Sins of Rory MacLeod

Lord Malcolm's Heart

Taming Lily

The Wicked Seduction of Wallace MacLeod

Love And Devotion

Wish Upon A Duke

Once Upon A Countess

Seduction of a Duke

Second Chance At Love

and w
stones. S
with

ABOUT THE AUTHOR

J. R. Salisbury is the historical romance alter-ego of contemporary romance author Jamie Salisbury. Writing romance stories with passion and sass, Jamie Salisbury has seen several of her books soar to #1 on Amazon. Her novella, Tudor Rubato was a finalist in the 2012 RONE awards. The cover won for Best Contemporary Cover. In 2014, her novel, Life and Lies was nominated for a RONE in the Erotica category. Her books are self published.

Music, traveling and history are among her passions when not writing. Her previous career in public relations in and around the entertainment field has afforded her with a treasure trove of endless story ideas.

Follow Jamie:
Book + Main
Website